SVEN CARTER
& THE TRASHMOUTH EFFECT

SVEN CARTER

& THE TRASHMOUTH EFFECT

ROB VLOCK

ALADDIN MAX

NEW YORK   LONDON   TORONTO   SYDNEY   NEW DELHI

ALADDIN MAX
Simon & Schuster Children's Publishing Division
1230 Avenue of the Americas, New York, New York 10020
First Aladdin MAX edition October 2017
Text copyright © 2017 by Rob Vlock
Cover illustration copyright © 2017 by Steven Scott
Also available in an Aladdin hardcover edition.
For information about special discounts for bulk purchases, please contact
Simon & Schuster Special Sales at 1-866-506-1949 or business@simonandschuster.com.
The Simon & Schuster Speakers Bureau can bring authors to your live event.
For more information or to book an event contact the Simon & Schuster Speakers Bureau
at 1-866-248-3049 or visit our website at www.simonspeakers.com.
Cover designed by Karin Paprocki
Interior designed by Mike Rosamilia
The text of this book was set in Adobe Caslon Pro.
Manufactured in the United States of America 0917 OFF
2 4 6 8 10 9 7 5 3 1
This book has been cataloged with the Library of Congress.
ISBN 978-1-4814-9014-6 (hc)
ISBN 978-1-4814-9013-9 (pbk)
ISBN 978-1-4814-9015-3 (eBook)

For Joey, Max, and Immy.

My three everythings.

CONTENTS

CHAPTER 1.0:
\ < value= [All Four Limbs Are Supposed to Remain Attached, Right?] \ >

"SVEN, THIS IS STUPID," WILL SAID FOR the millionth time.

And for the millionth time I ignored him.

We slowed to a stop in front of what used to be the entrance to the old Mad Skillz and Spillz Skate Park. Weeds poked up here and there through cracks in the pavement and graffiti covered nearly every surface. Plus, it smelled like burned rubber and rotten eggs. But it would do.

I yanked on the rusty, chained-up gate. Even Will wasn't skinny enough to fit through there.

"Seriously, dude," Will complained, "you know why they closed this place, right? About fifty kids got messed up big-time going over the Wreckinator. Remember? That high school kid fell so hard, his legs actually got driven up through his body. Everyone called him Flatfoot McStumpy after that."

"That's so not true," I insisted. "His head got pushed down into his shoulders. And they didn't call him Flatfoot McStumpy. It was Flathead McShorty."

"Whatever. The point is it's dangerous. Besides, it's closed. We shouldn't go in."

I found a section of fence that had rusted away from its post. I pulled it back. "Doesn't look closed to me." I carefully lifted the *item* out of the milk crate attached to my bike. Then I squeezed through the fence.

"Sven," Will moaned. "This is a really bad idea."

I gently placed the *item* on the ground right in front of the Wreckinator, the biggest ramp in the place.

"Come on." I grinned as I got my bike and wheeled it through the fence. "It's going to be epic. Just make sure you video it, okay? We'll probably get a billion hits on

YouTube! And when we're YouTube celebrities, people will forget we're the biggest losers in Schenectady. It's called street cred. Look it up."

I pedaled about fifty feet away and turned around, psyching myself up to make the jump. Will pulled out his phone to record my awesome stunt and started fretfully touching a metal railing over and over again with each of his fingers in turn: thumb, index finger, middle finger, ring finger, pinkie, and back again the other way. It made me anxious just watching him.

That was Will's thing, though. He had what doctors call obsessive-compulsive disorder. OCD, for short. And it made him, well ... a little different from most kids you might meet. When he got out of bed in the morning, he had to fold his blanket over four times, then make sure both his feet touched the floor at the same time at exactly 7:04. And then he would only leave his room after flicking the lights on and off forty-seven times.

Between that, his flaming red hair, and his immensely big hands (they were about the size of Frisbees), he kind of stood out. At our school, standing out wasn't something you wanted to do.

Maybe that's what made Will my best friend—and why he'd held the spot for the last seven years. We were both weird. I met him in this thing called the OCD Lunch Bunch at school and we really clicked. He never teased me for my, um . . . *unusual* eating habits. And, unlike everyone else at school, I never called him "Weird Willy."

I tried to tune out Will's railing tapping and turned my attention back to the jump. Just before I started pedaling toward the Wreckinator, a pair of crows landed on the rim of a corroded garbage barrel about ten feet away and stared at me with their shiny black eyes. Their inky feathers were so dark, they seemed to swallow up the crisp April sunlight that fell on them. I hesitated. I remembered reading somewhere that crows were bad luck.

"Shoo!" I yelled at the birds.

They didn't move.

"What?" I called with a shrug. "You've never seen

a kid jump over a three-layer wedding cake on his bike before?"

Yes, the *item* was a wedding cake. Not just any cake, though. It was a cake my mom baked. Which meant it ranked right up there with some of the greatest horrors the world had ever known. I preferred to call it "item" instead of "cake," since "cake" suggested something that was edible. This *item*? Definitely not fit for human consumption. But really cool to jump your bike over and earn some serious Internet fame. At least that was the plan.

The crows kept staring. I stuck my tongue out at them.

Will shouted, "Dude, are you having a conversation with those birds? 'Cause that's . . . a little odd."

"No! I'm just trying to, you know, psych myself up for the big jump."

I realized I was stalling. Because when I took a good look at that cake, yeah, it was pretty big. Three feet tall, at least. Not including the little plastic bride and groom perched on top.

I sucked in a big lungful of air. *You can do this*, I told

myself. And with one last glance at those stupid birds, I took off toward the ramp.

Wind whooshed past my ears with a low, ominous moan as I pumped my legs and picked up speed. My heart pounded against my rib cage and a drop of nervous sweat trickled down the back of my neck. Time ground to a crawl as I closed in on the Wreckinator.

With each slow second that ticked by, my fear grew, until, when I reached the foot of the ramp, the cake loomed like a hideously decorated three-story house.

My stomach lurched with the sudden change in trajectory as my tires rolled over the scarred surface of the Wreckinator, lifting me higher and higher toward the lip of the ramp. I caught a brief glimpse of Will, holding up his phone to film me from what felt like a thousand feet below. Was the air thinner up here, or was it just me forgetting to breathe altogether?

And that's when I realized . . .

I should have stopped.

I really, *really* should have stopped.

But it was too late.

My wheels left the solid concrete behind and spun uselessly in the air as my bike and I tried to defy gravity just long enough to clear the cake.

At first, I thought I was going to do it.

Then I noticed that the cake still seemed awfully far away.

Then I realized I wasn't so much flying over the cake as falling into it.

Then I knew this wasn't going to be epic at all.

My front wheel entered the cake at the precise place where the third layer met the second. And even though my mom's cakes had the approximate density of lead, they were no match for a kid on a bike plummeting down to Earth at face-peeling-off speeds from the top of the Wreckinator.

There was an explosion of frosting as the cake burst into a million little pieces. (Some of it might have even gotten into my mouth. *YUCK*!) But I couldn't worry about that, because I still had a chance to nail the landing.

You can do this, Sven! You can do this!

Except I couldn't.

All thanks to that stupid plastic bride and groom from the top of the cake.

They wedged themselves right into the spokes of my front wheel so that as soon as my bike made contact with the ground, it stopped dead.

But I didn't stop.

I continued on, straight over my handlebars, over the shattered remains of the cake and on through the air. I was flying. Until a split second later, when I slammed into the ground.

Will jogged up to where I lay sprawled out on the concrete, still recording me on his phone. "Dude! Are you all right?"

Dazed, I looked up at him and blinked a few times. Normally, you'd expect a question like that to be simple— either you're all right or you're not all right. You know, ballpoint pen sticking out of eyeball: not all right. Eating big bowl of ice cream: all right. Crocodile jaws slamming shut on head . . . well, you get the idea.

But at that moment, I honestly had to give it some serious thought. I wasn't dead, so that was good. No pens or other sharp objects stuck out of either one of my eyes. And I wasn't lying in a pool of blood.

"I think I'm okay. I guess I didn't make it?"

Will shook his head. "Not even close."

He reached down and grabbed my arm to help me up. "You're right, though. This'll get a billion hits on YouTube. Man, when you were flying through the air I thought for sure you were goi . . ."

I don't think he actually meant to say "goi." It's just that was what happened to be halfway out of Will's mouth when he lost the ability to speak.

I looked up at him. In his hand Will held something kind of flesh-colored and about the length of my arm. Which made perfect sense, since it was . . .

MY ARM!!! AND IT WASN'T ATTACHED TO MY BODY!!!

CHAPTER 2.0:
\ < value= [My Arm Takes a Walk] \ >

I LOOKED DOWN AT MY LEFT SHOULDER.
All I saw was an empty sleeve. But with Will screaming and all the blood soaking my shirt, it didn't take me long to understand what had happened—the crash had ripped off my arm!

"Aaaaggghhhhh!" screamed Will, flailing my arm in distress. "AAAAGGGGHHHH!!!"

I didn't know what he was screaming about. *I* was the kid whose arm was six feet away from the rest of his body. As I watched Will shaking my arm like some kind of meat maraca, I started screaming as well.

And then the pain hit.

"Oh my God!" I cried, clenching my teeth in agony. "My arm! Will, call nine-one-one!"

"Aaaaagggghhhhhh!" he replied.

"Will!" I tried again.

His answer was the same. "Aaaagggghhh!"

"Will, listen! Use your phone and call nine-one-one! Hurry!"

Will's scream faded to a moan, then a whimper. He took a deep breath, swallowed hard, and finally regained the ability to speak.

"Okay," he said. "Nine-one-one—I can do that. I think. How do I do that?" He looked at me with a blank expression. I think he was in shock.

"Just give me the phone! Give me the phone!" I screamed.

Will tossed the phone at me like it was a live electric eel. It tumbled through the air, bounced painfully off my head, and landed facedown on the asphalt.

"Why did you do that?" I growled, clenching my teeth against the agonizing throbbing that radiated from my shoulder, arcing across my entire chest.

"You said to give you the phone."

"I didn't say throw it at my head!" I picked up the phone. A tangle of cracks covered the blackened screen. "Will! You broke it!"

He looked like he was about to cry. "I—I—I—"

"Just go get my parents!" I said as calmly as I could manage. Which wasn't very calm at all. More like hysterical. My vision flickered as pain and panic tightened their viselike grip. "Hurry!"

Will trained his wild eyes on me, nodded slowly, then proceeded to lie on the ground and curl into the fetal position. That was what he did whenever he started freaking out.

"Will! Get up! You need to go for help! Please! Will!"

I finally must have gotten through to him, because he stopped rocking back and forth and rose unsteadily to his feet. Then he stumbled toward his bike.

"Wait!" I shouted after him.

"What?"

"Can you, um . . . you know . . . leave me my arm?"

Will must have forgotten what was in his hand,

because he suddenly turned even paler. He scampered over to me, holding the limb out like it was a dead rat or something (which, honestly, was kind of insulting) and placed it gingerly on my lap. Then he jumped on his bike and rode off, leaving me alone with my thoughts.

And my arm. It was surprisingly heavy and warm. And gross.

I wanted to look away from it, but I couldn't. The idea that this thing in my lap was a part of me, with all the veins and stringy bits of stuff hanging out of it . . . yuck! I couldn't wrap my head around it. I never really thought about what I looked like on the inside. But I decided I preferred how I looked on the outside.

Frantic thoughts buzzed around inside my skull like a swarm of angry hornets as I sat on the cool, rough pavement. Was I going to die? Would doctors be able to reattach my arm? What would happen if I wanted to become a professional juggler?

Just then my arm did something unexpected.

It twitched.

Then it seemed to wave at me.

Then it started flopping around like a dying fish.

It flopped right out of my lap and fell with a slap onto the pavement.

In a moment, it began dragging itself toward me using its fingers—*my* fingers—like little legs.

My skin went all cold and sweaty as I watched my arm dragging itself across the ground.

"No, no, no!" I screamed at the arm, terrified beyond the point of reason. "Stop doing that!"

I watched in horror as the arm grabbed the bottom of my shirt and managed to hoist itself halfway up my side. It paused for a second, just hanging there.

"Get off! Down!" I commanded.

It didn't listen. Instead, it did a graceful little flip so that its bloody end slapped with a wet *smack* right back onto my shoulder.

That's when everything went black.

CHAPTER 3.0:
\ < value= [It All Started with a Cake] \ >

SO, HOW DID I END UP LYING ON THE cracked pavement of an old skate park, temporarily missing an arm, covered in the world's nastiest baked good?

You can thank my mom for that.

You see, making cakes was a second career for my mom. Well, technically it was a sixth career. Right after she got fired from her job at the real estate agency. Before that she was a photographer. And before that, a website designer, a sculptor, and a landscape architect. She always said she just had to find her thing.

Cakes weren't her thing.

Take, for example, the cake that I had tried to jump over. It looked like it had been molded out of white papier-mâché by a six-year-old. A blind six-year-old. With hooks for hands. Which was why, a couple of hours earlier, the woman Mom had baked it for refused to pay for it, screamed, "Thanks for ruining my wedding," and slammed the door behind her as she stormed out of the house.

But if there was one thing about Mom's cakes, it was that their ugliness was way more than skin deep. As bad as they looked, they tasted far, far worse.

Everything she baked was "trendsetting." Those were her words, not mine. The words I would have chosen would have been "vomit-inducing." Because lima beans and basil were never meant to go into cakes. Or orange slices and tuna. And definitely not garlic, mint, and curry. It was like she had a gift for making things taste bad. Only it wasn't so much a gift as a horrible, nightmarish curse.

So when Mom ended up with an entire disgusting wedding cake and no wedding to send it to, I smuggled it out of the house when she wasn't looking, got Will, and pedaled over to the skate park to use it as a prop in my sure-to-be-a-megahit YouTube stunt. The rest you know. I crash, my arm comes off and reattaches itself. Then I pass out.

And that's where my dad came in.

"Sven!"

I slowly opened my eyes.

"Sven!"

A blurry shape hovering over me drifted into focus. A face. A squashed-up nose. Tight-set mouth. Nostril hair practically long enough to braid. I'd know that nostril hair anywhere.

"What are you doing sitting on the ground?" Dad barked gruffly.

"I, uh—"

"And what in the name of Joe Namath's jockstrap are you doing covered in cake?"

My dad, Alexander "Big Al" Carter, stood a couple of inches over five feet tall. But to say he was a small man would be dead wrong. Well, technically it would be right.

He *was* a small man. But he *acted* like a big man. It was his way of making up for being so very little.

Being small was the worst thing that had ever happened to my dad. Because, from the time he was a toddler, all he ever wanted to do was become a professional football player. But he was never big enough.

That was bad for him.

And probably even worse for me.

Because Dad wanted nothing more than to make me an all-American football star. Sometimes I wondered if that was why he and Mom had adopted me. Every day he'd wake me up at five thirty to practice throwing a stupid football through a stupid tire he hung from a tree in the backyard while he'd yell, "You can't throw to save your life! Lift your elbow next time! Extend your arm! You're not rotating enough! Your strumfobbler needs to be level with your fartwaddles!"

He probably didn't actually say that last one. But he may as well have, for all the good his coaching did. No matter how much we practiced, no matter what we tried, I just never got any better. I'd get the ball through the tire once in a while. And I'd miss a whole lot. I stank. And we'd repeat the whole stupid exercise the next morning. *Every* morning.

So it didn't surprise me a bit to hear that the next words out of my father's mouth were: "How's your throwing arm?"

Still too freaked-out to explain, I just made a sort of lame croaking sound.

He squinted at me. "Are you okay, son? Your friend told me your arm fell off. Is that some kind of new slang you kids are using these days? Like, 'that party was so the bomb that my arm fell off'?"

I found my words. "No! My arm actually came off! It did! Only then it went back on! And now it's on and not off but it was off before it was on!"

Even I didn't know what I was talking about.

For a few seconds, he looked at me like I was some kind of lunatic. Then he marched over to me and pulled up my sleeve.

"Hmm," he grunted. "I've seen worse. Move your arm."

"Dad," I protested, "I can't! What if it falls off again?"

"Sven," he insisted, "quit kidding around. Move your arm."

I ventured a glance at my left arm. I wasn't sure what I'd see there.

My arm was right where it was supposed to be. On my shoulder. Just like it always had been.

Had I dreamed the whole arm-coming-off-then-coming-alive-and-climbing-up-my-shirt-and-reattaching-itself thing? Maybe I went into shock or something and it had all been a hallucination. But where it had reattached itself, a deep red band of raw flesh ran clear around my shoulder. It hadn't been a dream!

"Dad," I cried. "Look! This is where my arm fell off! See? Really! It did!"

A look of concern spread across my dad's face. "Um, Sven? You didn't happen to hit your *head*, did you?"

"No, my head's fine! My arm fell off! It's . . . Just take me to the hospital, okay? So they can fix it and we can . . ."

I trailed off as I noticed the way my dad was looking at me. He obviously thought I was crazy. Maybe he was right. I mean, noncrazy people didn't usually see their arms come off, then crawl back into place and reattach themselves. Did they?

Dad ran his fingers through his thinning hair. "You know, son, maybe you're right. We probably should have a doctor check you out. But I'll be Tom Brady's tutu if I'm going to spend all night in a hospital waiting room. I'll call Dr. Shallix instead."

I had a feeling he was more worried about my sanity than my arm.

Dad helped me to my feet, pulled a handkerchief out of his pocket, and used it to wipe as much cake off my bike as he could. Then he loaded the bike into the back of his beige minivan. While he was doing that, I noticed Will's phone lying on the pavement, so I picked it up and slipped it into my pocket.

A few minutes later, we were driving toward the doctor's office.

CHAPTER 4.0:
\ < value= [Please Don't Call Me Trashmouth] \ >

I WAS A LITTLE DISAPPOINTED THAT HE was taking me to Dr. Shallix instead of to the hospital. For two reasons. First, even though he had been my doctor for my whole life, that dude still seriously weirded me out every time I saw him. Second, I kind of *wanted* to go to the hospital for once. Just to see what it was like. I know that probably sounds bizarre. But I had never been to one before. Heck, I had never even been sick in my life. Literally *never*. Not a cold, not a cough, not a sniffle. And that was yet one more reason I felt like a complete and total weirdo.

You see, there's something you should know about

me—something I haven't wanted to mention until now. I was always a little strange compared to, well . . . just about every other kid at school. Or on the planet, for that matter. At least that's how it felt.

Why? Because I ate things. Gross things.

Chewed-up gum from underneath movie theater seats. Cockroaches. That brown stuff that kept growing on the side of the fish tank no matter how clean I tried to keep the water.

And when I came across gross things I couldn't eat, I'd lick them. Like the nozzles of water fountains and the poles people hold on to on the bus.

Don't get me wrong. I never liked doing these things. I found eating them just as disgusting as you probably find hearing about them. It's just that I . . . had to. I couldn't help myself.

You know how when you're at a party and there's a big bowl of potato chips sitting right in front of you and you can't help eating pretty much all of them? It was just like that for me every day. Only, instead of potato chips, it was used tissues and old eggshells and about a thousand other things no normal kid would ever want to eat. It was like my mouth had a mind of its own.

I had always tried to keep this habit secret. I might not have been able to stop myself, but at least I could keep other people from seeing it. For a long time, nobody knew anything about it. Unfortunately, that all changed the day I ate a moldy, dust-bunny-covered blueberry muffin I found under the bleachers in gym.

I tried to make sure nobody saw me. But right after I stuffed the muffin into my mouth, I looked up to see Brandon Marks staring right at me. After that, I was known as Trashmouth. Brandon made it up. And he did everything he could to get the whole school to call me that.

Just my luck, the problem got a whole lot worse whenever I was nervous or stressed. At the precise moment I needed to look like a dude who had his act together, I'd need a taste of the gray sludge from the janitor's bucket more than I needed oxygen. Before a big test, I'd lick the top of my desk when nobody was looking. If I was talking to a pretty girl, I'd have an uncontrollable urge to eat a handful of dirt from a nearby potted plant. Which never did much to impress pretty girls.

My parents knew about this little habit of mine, of course. It's kind of tough to keep something like that secret from your mom and dad. Especially when every time they'd take me to the dentist, I'd end up eating a bunch of those cotton things they stuff in people's mouths. I'd fish used ones out of the garbage can next to the dentist's chair whenever she would turn her back to pick up an instrument.

"Oh, that's just Sven being Sven. He's fine," Mom would always say when Dad mentioned that he caught me eating yellow snow or scarfing down a dead worm I picked out of a puddle or licking dried bird droppings off the car's windshield.

"Hmmmph," Dad would scoff, shaking his head and rolling his eyes. "When most people find a Band-Aid in their soup, they send it back."

"Come on, Dad," I'd argue. "That only happened once. And it wasn't soup, it was chili."

Then Dad would sigh and rub his temples with the

tips of his fingers, the way he always did when I disappointed him.

Eating gross stuff never made me sick or anything, though. So Dr. Shallix said they shouldn't worry about it. That I'd outgrow it eventually. And yet there I was, more than ten years later, still drawn to clumps of cat litter like a fruit fly to overripe bananas. (That was why we didn't have a cat anymore.)

And all the while my social life went right down the toilet. I mean, I was in seventh grade. Chester A. Arthur Middle School. Home of the Fighting Lungfish, Upstate New York's third-best middle school water polo team. Anyway, at CLAMS—that's what we called our school for short (I don't know where the *L* came from)—if you weren't popular, you were no one.

I was no one.

Will had a theory about why I never got sick. He said he thought all the gross stuff I ate gave me kind of a superhuman immune system. Like my body got so used to dealing with all the germs I was putting in my mouth that a regular old cold virus wouldn't stand a chance.

Maybe. It wasn't a bad theory. I mean, it would explain why I had never had so much as a runny nose in my life. I had never even sneezed before. Not once. Ever.

But whether or not his theory was right, the fact that I had never experienced what it was like to sneeze made me feel like even more of a freak.

Just once I wanted to get sick. Nothing terrible. Just a cold. Or maybe the flu. Not only so I could take a day off from school for the first time ever, but so I could know how it felt to be like everybody else, instead of, as usual, some strange kid who never sneezed.

CHAPTER 5.0:
\ < value= [My Weird Doctor Wants to Kill Me] \ >

DR. SHALLIX WAS ALREADY WAITING FOR us when we got to his office. He hadn't bothered to turn on any of the lights in the office, and in the gloom I could see his teeth illuminated by the glow of a streetlight outside. The overall effect was creepy as anything. Even worse than that time I looked in Will's grandma's underwear drawer on a dare.

The doctor flipped the light switch on the wall and a row of fluorescent tubes flickered on overhead.

That was a bit better. But I was still creeped out.

Dr. Shallix was a thin man, about sixty years old, with a thick, bristly tuft of white hair sticking up from his oversize head. His big noggin, coarse white hair, and scrawny body reminded me a little of the scrub brush my mom used to clean the toilet. The toilet brush never put an ice-cold stethoscope on my chest or told me to turn my head and cough while touching me you-know-where, though.

His teeth were a little too big and a little too white, and he was always smiling this huge perma-smile of his. I mean, *always*. Even though he never really seemed all that happy.

Dr. Shallix had an accent I could never quite figure out. It might have been German or French, or maybe Russian. Whatever it was, he always spoke in a soft, reassuring way—a little too slowly, ending most of his sentences by asking, "Yes?" as if he thought you were a baby and wanted to make sure you understood everything before moving on to his next point. His voice never actually reassured me, though. More like gave me the willies.

"Now, Sven." Dr. Shallix smiled. "Let us take a look at that arm of yours. Mr. Carter, you will stay here in the waiting room, yes?"

Dad had already settled into a vinyl-upholstered chair and started thumbing through an issue of *Overbearing Parent Magazine*, so he just nodded distractedly.

Dr. Shallix led me down the hall toward the examination rooms. Over the years, I had visited each of them at one time or another when I had my annual checkups. They were all decorated for little kids. The first had pictures of kittens and bunnies. The second was plastered with decals of race cars with stupid faces on them. And the third was basically one big mural of a monkey that was either singing or throwing up a bunch of musical notes it had just eaten. We went into that one.

"Hop up," Dr. Shallix said, patting the examination table.

I climbed uncertainly onto the table.

"Now, you will take off your shirt so we can get a good look at that arm, yes?"

I hesitated. I hated taking my shirt off in front of people. I had a birthmark on the left side of my chest, just about where I figured my heart was. It looked like a pale red *O* about the size of my fist. I'd never seen anyone else with one like it. It felt like yet another reminder that I was different from everybody else.

"Come on, now," Dr. Shallix chided. "Do not be shy. I am a doctor, yes?"

I slid my shirt off over my head, wincing as the fabric dragged across my shoulder.

"Hmm . . . the shoulder always seems to be the weak point," Dr. Shallix muttered to himself, smiling as he studied my arm. "External regeneration seems within specifications, however."

He poked at the raw, red injury with a shiny, pointy metal thing.

"Ouch!" I gasped.

Dr. Shallix nodded. "Good."

I failed to see what was so good about it.

He picked up an instrument that looked like an oversize metal hairbrush and held it over my shoulder. It didn't look like any medical device I'd ever seen before— even on all those real-life emergency room shows that Mom and Dad didn't like me watching. It beeped a few times and displayed some numbers on a little screen in the handle.

"Circulatory systems are functioning normally." He paused to open up a sleek silver laptop and clicked open a window that read S. CARTER—OMICRON PROTOCOL at the top. When he saw me looking at the screen, he angled the laptop away from me and typed a few notes into it. Finally, he closed it up and looked at me again. "Now, Sven, you will tell me what happened, yes?"

I didn't know what to say. Telling him I thought I had a detachable arm like some kind of flesh-and-blood LEGO guy would probably get me sent to the loony bin. So I started to make up a more believable story. "Um, you see, there was this kitten stuck in a tree, and I—"

"The truth would be better," he remarked matter-of-factly, his teeth glinting. "You can tell me what really happened. After all, I am your doctor, yes?"

I kept my mouth shut.

"It is okay, Sven. Whatever you say will just be between us, yes? I simply want to understand what happened so I can be sure you are not . . . seriously damaged. After all, we need you shipshape for your thirteenth birthday. It is just this Saturday, yes?"

He smiled at me in a way that said he wouldn't take no for an answer. So I took a deep breath and told him everything.

When I finished my story, Dr. Shallix stared at me for a few moments, scratching his chin. Finally, he spoke.

"I think I see what has happened here. You *believe* you saw your arm amputated. But that is just the trauma talking, yes? The brain plays tricks on us sometimes. The shock, the distress of having an accident, can alter your perceptions. You scraped your shoulder pretty badly, I can see that. But obviously your arm is still attached, yes? You just imagined something else happened. Do you understand this?"

No. I didn't understand. There was no way I imagined it. I *felt* the pain of my arm pulling away from my body. I *saw* Will holding my arm out like a dead thing. I *heard* him screaming. Why would Will be screaming if all I'd done was scrape up my shoulder?

A wave of anger swelled inside me. How dare he tell me that what happened hadn't happened?

"You're wrong!" I spat. "I know what happened! And it wasn't my imagination!"

"Please, Sven. Be reasonable," oozed Dr. Shallix in his most soothing voice. "Surely, you must understand what you are telling me is impossible, yes?"

"I know it's impossible," I snapped through gritted teeth. "But it happened anyway."

He shook his head. "It is impossible."

This was like banging my head against a brick wall. How could I get him to listen to me?

I remembered Will's phone.

"Here!" I cried. "I'll show you!"

I pulled the phone out of my back pocket and tried to turn it on. The shattered screen flickered a couple of times and went black. *Ugh!*

"I do not understand. You have a nonfunctional telephonic device, yes?" Dr. Shallix said quietly.

"Yeah," I replied, "well, this nonfunctional telephonic device recorded the whole thing! My arm came off! You can see it yourself. I mean, you could if the phone was working."

Dr. Shallix smiled and tut-tutted me. Then he pried the phone from my hand. "Sven, do you not see you are deceiving yourself into believing this absurd fantasy? That is not good for a growing boy's psyche, yes?"

He dropped the phone into a trash can next to the exam table.

"Hey!" I objected.

"Now, now. That is the best place for it. The sooner you forget about this delusion, the better off you will be, yes?"

"Stop telling me it's a delusion! It's not a delusion!" I screamed. "You know what? You can just ask my friend, Will. He was there. He saw the whole thing. Just ask him!"

A grim expression spread across Dr. Shallix's face for just a moment, and then the smile returned. "Ah, yes. Will. He saw it. Well, then, that changes things."

He stroked his chin again, lost in thought for a few seconds.

"Yes, that changes things. Very unfortunate, yes? I had hoped it would not come to this."

He smiled when he said it. But his words sent a cold bolt of lightning shooting down my spine.

As I watched him slide open a drawer on the front of the exam table, I wondered what he meant by "I had hoped it would not come to this." In the movies, bad guys would say something like that just before they—

Dr. Shallix pulled something out of the drawer. It was a . . . a huge, curved, deadly-looking knife!

CHAPTER 6.0:
\ < value= [Meat Loaf, Brussels Sprouts, and Misery] \ >

SORRY. IT TURNS OUT I MIGHT HAVE BEEN overreacting a little. What I thought was a knife was a pair of scissors. Dr. Shallix wrapped my shoulder tightly in a clean, white bandage and used the scissors to snip off the excess gauze. Then he put them away.

A wave of relief washed over me.

Until Dr. Shallix put his hand on my good shoulder and squeezed. Hard.

His voice had a threatening quality, despite his too-wide smile. "I want you to do something for me, Sven, yes? First, keep this bandage on your arm for at least a week. Until you are fully healed. A *week*. Do you under-stand?"

I swallowed hard and nodded. I was afraid to do any-thing else.

"Second," he continued, "I want you to promise you will not speak about any of this *nonsense* with anybody. Not your parents. Not your friends. It is not good for you to indulge this fantasy of yours. It could lead to lasting psychological problems, yes? The kind of problems a boy could be . . . institutionalized for. You understand what that means, yes?"

I nodded again. "It means the nuthouse, right?"

Dr. Shallix's smile grew until it seemed almost wider than his head. "But we will make sure it does not come to that, yes, Sven? I know your parents would be so sad to have you taken from them. For your own good, of course. All of this is for your own good, Sven. So let us agree that we will never mention your fantastic story again, yes?"

"Yeah, okay. I guess it's a pretty crazy story," I said, because that seemed like the safest thing to say. I forced out a laugh. It sounded hollow.

When we got to the waiting room, I immediately slumped into a chair. My legs felt like they were made of that stuff that passes for pudding in the school cafeteria. My stomach clenched into a tight knot. I was freaking out. I didn't know whether to run out of there or hide in the coat closet.

Instead, I licked the side of the fish tank next to me.

"Hey there, champ." Dad smiled in a way-too-chipper way when he saw me. "How's the arm? You doing okay?"

Before I could answer, Dr. Shallix responded.

"He is fine, Mr. Carter. Just a little scrape on the shoulder, yes? You probably will not even know it was there in a week or so. But he has been worried that the injury is far worse than it really is. So please call me if he continues to talk about this delusion of his. And I will . . ."

He shot me a glance.

". . . and I will be sure to take care of the problem."

"Sure, Doc," my dad said in a distracted sort of way. "Yeah, yeah. Anything unusual. Got it. Sven, you ready to go?"

Dad rocked back and forth on his heels impatiently. I

took a step toward him, but Dr. Shallix stopped me, placing his hand on the back of my neck. He squeezed hard enough to let me know he wasn't above hurting a kid, then smiled down at me.

"Take care of that shoulder and remember what we discussed, yes?"

My Creep-O-Meter™ went totally off the charts. I mean, this dude was always sort of creepy. But now? He was like creepy times a million.

I nodded, because what else was I going to do?

His smile broadened just a bit and he let me go.

As soon as I stepped into the house, Mom started covering my face with wet kisses.

Yuck!

She smelled like bananas and soy sauce. Obviously, she had been baking something. And I thought I knew what. A shudder shot through me.

"Oh, my brave little man!" she cried. "Are you okay? What did the doctor say?"

"I'm fine, Mom," I said, wiping her saliva off my face.

"Your father told me you thought your arm fell off."

I scratched the back of my neck. "Uh, well, you see—"

Dad cut me off. "Dr. Shallix told me that it was . . . what did he call it? A *delusion*. You know . . ." He traced circles in the air next to his temple and whistled.

"Dad!" I objected. "I'm not crazy!"

"Of course not, son. No one's saying you're crazy. Just . . . delusional."

"Well," Mom chirped. "I'm just glad you're home. I made your favorites for dinner. Banana soy meat loaf with maple-glazed Brussels sprouts."

"Oh. Thanks, Mom."

Needless to say, banana soy meat loaf and maple-glazed Brussels sprouts weren't my favorites. I hated them. But somehow my mom had gotten it into her head that I loved them, and I didn't have the heart to tell her how disgusting they were. But on the bright side, at least she hadn't made me a cake.

All through dinner, Dad kept shooting me these looks, like he thought I was about to do something insane. The only thing I did, though, was poke halfheartedly at the "food" on my plate, choking down a few bites for my mom's sake. But I had no appetite. And not just because the meal was revolting—I felt sick with anxiety and fear.

I plucked a dead fly from the windowsill behind me and scarfed it down.

My father sighed loudly. "He's happy to eat dead bugs, but will he eat perfectly good food? No!"

"Dr. Shallix said we're not supposed to make a big deal about it, Al," Mom said in a half whisper.

"What does he know?" Dad countered. "He also said he'd grow out of it. Does it look like he's grown out of it?"

"Um, I think I'll turn in early tonight," I said. I wasn't really tired, but I couldn't stand sitting there listening to the usual argument about how weird I was.

My parents were too busy debating my strangeness to even notice I had left the table.

When I got into bed, I knew there was no chance I was going to be able to sleep. I stared at the ceiling for what must have been hours, thinking about all the weird stuff that had happened. Finally, I got out of bed and flipped on the light.

Dr. Shallix had told me to leave the gauze on my shoulder for at least a week. But I didn't care. Everyone telling me I was crazy was, well, driving me crazy! I couldn't stand it anymore! I had to know whether there was something under the bandage that would explain what had happened.

Standing in front of the mirror on the back of my bedroom door, I started to unwrap the bandage. I slowly uncoiled one layer of gauze after another until . . .

What I saw practically knocked the breath right out of me.

There was nothing there. I mean, there was a shoulder, of course. But nothing else. No injury. No scar. Nothing. No evidence whatsoever that I had hurt myself at all.

I touched my shoulder. The skin felt perfectly smooth. And it didn't hurt anymore. I dug around in my desk until I found the Li'l Explorers magnifying glass I had gotten for my eighth birthday. Even looking through that, I couldn't see anything. Not a scratch.

It was like it never happened.

CHAPTER 7.0:
\ < value= [The Science of Bullying] \ >

CHESTER A. ARTHUR MIDDLE SCHOOL
was pretty much like any other middle school—filled with
a whole bunch of eleven-, twelve-, and thirteen-year-old
students who had the lethal aim of a heat-seeking missile
when it came to searching out and humiliating kids who
were different. In other words, for someone like me, it
was pure misery. And that was on a good day.

This was not a good day.

For one thing, I couldn't get my shoulder off my
mind. I had been so sure I'd find something to prove
my story when I unwrapped that bandage. Maybe I *was*
going crazy.

But no! I knew I wasn't crazy. I *knew* it!

Something weird was going on here. And it wasn't all in my head.

Just a couple of months earlier, I fell off my bike and scraped my knee. I had a big scab that took weeks to heal. And that was nowhere near as bad as an arm getting ripped off. So where was the scab? Where was the scar? Even Dad had seen *something* there.

I sat through homeroom, staring blankly at the whiteboard, going through every detail of what had happened the day before. The cake. The jump. My arm crawling around by itself. Will's phone bouncing off my head.

Wait! Will's phone! If I could somehow get it working, I could watch the video and prove I wasn't crazy!

But there was no way Dr. Shallix would give it back to me. He'd just say I was imagining things. Then he'd send me to the nuthouse.

It was hopeless.

The thought was so consuming, I barely had enough brain space left over to worry about Brandon Marks.

Brandon Marks, by the way, was the second thing that made that day particularly sucky.

Then again, Brandon Marks made pretty much every day particularly sucky, so I guess it was kind of par for the course.

It all started during first period. Science class. I kind of liked science. It was interesting. And our science teacher, Mr. Collins, was actually pretty cool. The only problem was we sat at these big black lab tables, and guess who always sat right behind me? Brandon Marks. Which meant every time we did some kind of experiment, I'd end up being on the receiving end of one of Brandon's pranks.

Over the last month alone, Brandon had drenched me with a vinegar-and-baking-soda volcano, dropped a live tadpole down the back of my pants, sprinkled hamster droppings in my hair, and unleashed the inhabitants of an entire ant farm into my backpack.

And that didn't even count all the prior years of psychological warfare he waged against me. Ever since our first class together in third grade, Brandon had done everything in his power to make me an outcast in everybody's eyes—and make me feel like the world's biggest misfit, the universe's ultimate outsider. *Trashmouth?* That was just the tip of the cruelty iceberg. A drop in the bullying bucket.

The worst thing about Brandon, though? I couldn't do anything about him. You see, his dad was my dad's boss at Spray-Yum Aerosolized Foods. If you've ever eaten food that you spray out of a can, there's a good chance my dad had something to do with it.

Anyway, having your worst enemy's father be your father's boss really sucks. Once I went to the vice principal to tell on Brandon. He got in trouble. The problem was, so did my dad. The next day, he got demoted from senior director of canification to flavor assurance engineer. That was a fancy way of saying he had to taste every batch of Spray-Yum's products before they got canned. Including their new Liver-'n'-Onion Krack'r Spread. Let's just say I've never seen Dad so unhappy. All because of me telling on Brandon.

In the end, what all this meant was I couldn't do a thing about Brandon, no matter what he did to me.

"Okay, kids," Mr. Collins said, looking out at the class through wire-rimmed glasses with lenses so thick they made his eyes look like tiny brown pebbles at the bottom of a pond. "Today I'm going to introduce you to the wonderful world of electromagnetism!"

Mr. Collins was always saying things in an exaggerated voice like that. Like he thought everything about science was megacool. Which, I guess, did make it kind of cool.

He yanked a big brown sheet off some kind of contraption sitting on his desk. It was made out of a whole bunch of wires and stuff that were plugged into the wall. "This, my friends, is an electromagnet that I built. It uses an iron core and about two hundred windings of copper wire to convert electrical energy into a magnetic field. So what can you do with it?"

He grabbed the handle of a round metal plate wrapped with wire, held it over a big bowl of paper clips, and flipped a switch. Instantly, hundreds of paper clips leapt out of the bowl and attached themselves to the plate. Then he turned the magnet off and the paper clips fell back into the bowl.

"Okay, kids," Mr. Collins called out to the class. "Pick

a lab partner and come up with a way you can tell me how many paper clips I was able to lift using this magnet, and how much they weigh."

I looked at the empty seat next to me. It was Will's. He was out that day. Probably taking what he liked to call a "mental health day." It was usually because of OCD-related things—like if he accidentally got up at 7:05 instead of 7:04—or if he was just feeling particularly anxious. Given what he had seen at the skate park yesterday, I wasn't surprised to see Will's seat completely devoid of Will. Which left me without a lab partner. Because no one other than Will would ever team up with me.

I looked around the room for a potential partner. But every set of eyes I made contact with quickly darted away from the weirdo boy. I mean, God forbid anybody get anywhere near the kid who might drink the juice out of a dissected frog or chomp down on a handful of owl pellets.

So before long, everyone else in the class had split off into pairs and was busily counting and weighing paper clips.

All except for me.

And Alicia Toth, of course.

She never had a lab partner.

Alicia had transferred to our school at the beginning of the year from somewhere in the Midwest or something. She never liked to talk about it, though. So she just said she was from nowhere. And nobody really cared enough to question it. She was the new girl, after all.

So while everyone else chose to work with a friend, she was, as usual, the odd person out.

Then again, it wasn't like she was trying to win over any friends. I had never seen her talk to anybody. It was almost as if she had set up some invisible barrier between herself and everybody else. A wall that kept her all alone in her own private universe. And as far as I could tell, that was the way she wanted it.

She must have been awfully lonely, though. I mean, Will may have been my one and only friend, but she had no one. I couldn't help but feel kind of bad for her.

I guess that's why I did what I did.

"Hey, uh, do you, um, you know, want to, uh, partner up for lab today?"

With her black, shoulder-length braids, skin so pale it was almost translucent, and vivid green eyes, she was really pretty. I thought so, anyway. Which made me seriously nervous. I was barely able to fight off the impulse to lick the black stone top of the lab table.

She peered at me with distrust for a moment, then slowly nodded. "Yeah, okay. I guess. Thanks."

I had never really met her properly before. Probably because she was always so unfriendly. At first, I thought she just seemed like the supercool type and kept to herself because she thought she was too awesome for everyone else, staring at people with those big, bright green eyes of hers and never saying a word.

But eventually, I came to see her as just another outsider like me. Maybe not as weird, but probably just as lonely. And some part of me always wished I could do something about that. There were never any cracks in her cold façade that I could use to get a foothold on conversation, though, so we never ended up talking. Not a single word.

Until today.

CHAPTER 8.0:
\ < value= [I Have a Magnetic Personality] \ >

"THIS IS DUMB," ALICIA MUTTERED, NOT exactly to me, but in my general direction.

"I know, right?" I quickly responded, trying to sound cool and not nervous, even though the opposite was true. "I mean, who cares? And it's not like you could figure it out anyway. You'd have to be some kind of superbrainiac."

Alicia flashed me a look that told me my effort to be cool just fell flat. "What are you talking about?"

"Uh, um, uh . . . ," I stammered, totally unprepared to actually have a conversation with a pretty girl. I could feel the blood rushing to my face. "Well, uh, everyone knows Mr. Collins always gives these impossible questions," I managed to say. "Um . . . so his students understand that, like, not having answers is part of science and that it's okay to fail and stuff."

"Seriously?" she yawned. "I could have done this in third grade."

I laughed because obviously she was joking.

She didn't laugh because apparently she wasn't joking. "He practically gave us the answer when he told us how many windings he used. To figure out the strength of a magnetic field you just have to multiply the number of turns of wire by the amperage of the power source. He told us it had two hundred windings, so assuming he's plugged into a twenty-amp wall outlet, that gives you four thousand gauss. That kind of magnetic density can lift about . . . half a pound of ferrous metal. Since standard paper clips weigh approximately one gram each, and there are four hundred fifty-three grams per pound, I'm going to say he lifted two hundred seventy-five clips."

I stared at her with my mouth hanging open.

"Okay, everybody," Mr. Collins said a few minutes later. "Since I'm sure no one got the right answer—which is fine, because in science you can always learn from your failures—I'll tell you how many paper clips I lifted. I counted them while you were working, and the answer is two hundred seventy-four."

My mouth hung even lower. "Why didn't you say something?"

She didn't answer and started bending a paper clip into a circle.

Mr. Collins spent the rest of the period showing us how, by winding more wire around the core, he could make the magnet stronger and stronger until he was able to lift up a twenty-pound dumbbell with it.

The whole time this was going on, I was waiting for Brandon to make his move. But he didn't. When the bell rang at the end of class, I breathed a sigh of relief—I had made it through a whole science class without Brandon doing a single nasty thing to me.

Only I spoke too soon. As we all filed out of class, Brandon dashed up to Mr. Collins's desk, picked up the electromagnet, flipped the switch, and stuck it in my face.

"Hey, eat this, Trashmouth," he guffawed. "Looks

like it's made out of a bunch of trash, so you'll love it! How's it taste?"

I couldn't answer him. Because at that moment, it felt like my face was being ripped right off my skull. The pain was excruciating. It was like a thousand fishhooks stuck themselves into every part of my face and then a thousand Olympic weight lifters started yanking on those fishhooks as hard as they could. Every cell in my head pulled in a different direction. I tried to open my mouth to scream, but it was like my lips were fused to the magnet.

Just as I was about to pass out from the pain, the magnet cut out and dropped away from my face, clattering to the floor.

Standing in front of me, her hand on the electromagnet's switch, was Alicia.

"You okay?" she asked.

"Uh, I don't know." I put my hands to my face to make sure it was still in one piece. My face felt like it had been sucked on by a gigantic vacuum cleaner, but at least it hadn't been torn off my head. "Yeah, I think," I panted.

Alicia looked at me with a curious expression. "What was that about?"

"The usual," I sighed. "Brandon Marks."

She squinted at me with her piercing green eyes. "No, I mean what happened with that magnet? It looked like it was . . . stuck to your face. You have braces or something?"

I showed her my teeth in what probably was more of a grimace than the smile I wanted it to be. "No, no braces. I . . . I have no idea what just happened. It felt like it was ripping my face off, though. Thanks for turning it off."

Without taking her eyes off me, she slowly reached into her backpack.

The bell for second period rang, and Mr. Collins's next class flooded into the room. Alicia paused, looked around, then took her hand out of her backpack and zipped it up.

"I'll see you later," she said abruptly.

She trotted out of the room to her second-period class, leaving me alone with the contraption that had tried to eat my face.

What had just happened? Had I gotten an electrical shock from the magnet? I gingerly reached out and touched the device, bracing myself for a zap. But my finger just met the cool copper wires. No shock. No pain. No nothing.

Hmm.

I reached out to turn the magnet back on.

"Sven?" Mr. Collins said when my finger was an inch away from the switch. "Don't you have a class to get to?"

"Oh, right. Yeah." I packed up my bag and headed out for second period, trying in vain to make sense of my run-in with the magnet.

CHAPTER 9.0:
\ < value= [I Commit a Felony] \ >

I WAITED THAT NIGHT UNTIL I HEARD MOM
and Dad engaging in their nightly symphony of snores
before I slipped out of bed and got dressed. I put on a
black shirt and the darkest jeans I had.

What I was about to do was probably the stupidest
thing I had ever done in my life—and that included jumping over the cake. But I needed Will's phone. I *needed* it.
Like, *needed* needed it. It was all I could think about.

Because if I couldn't prove that I wasn't insane, I'd
just . . . go crazy. And that phone was the one piece of
evidence that could show my arm really had come off. I
had to get it back.

So I slapped on my Fighting Lungfish baseball cap, pulled the brim down as low as I could, crept down the stairs, and snuck out of the house.

The streetlights cast a weak sepia glow as I approached Shallix Pediatrics on Union Street half an hour later. My guts felt like they were turning to jelly. Not just because I was about to do something about a million times more illegal than anything I had ever done, but because Schenectady was kind of creepy at night. Every alley I passed concealed dark shadows that seemed to move and rustle. As I walked, I thought I saw someone—or something—disappear around nearly every corner. Footsteps would echo behind me, but when I turned around, no one was there.

By the time I got to the front door of Dr. Shallix's office, my fear nearly made me chicken out. I couldn't believe I was about to do this. I wasn't a criminal. The worst thing I ever did before this was scarf down a few grapes in the produce section of the supermarket when my mom wasn't looking.

I glanced behind me to make sure nobody was around. The street was empty. So I tried the door. Locked. Of course. My heart sank. What had I expected? That Dr. Shallix would just leave the place open for anyone who might want to stop by at midnight?

I searched for another way in. The front of the building only had the door and a large plate-glass window. I decided to check out the alley to the right. A slanting shard of light from a streetlight provided just enough illumination for me to keep from walking face-first into a brick wall. I squinted against the darkness, looking for a way in.

Then I saw it. A small window about eight feet from the ground. It looked like it might have been left ajar.

But I couldn't reach it. If only I could find something to climb on. Like the Dumpster I proceeded to bang my knee against, for example, because I was busy looking up at the window. *Ouch!*

I was lucky it was positioned just below the window, because it was way too big for me to move by myself. I scrambled on top of it as quietly as I could. The overpowering stench of rotting garbage rising from it made my head spin. I almost fell in, but I regained my balance and nervously licked a film of Dumpster sludge off my finger. Then I pulled myself up to the window. It slid open smoothly, and a second later I hoisted myself onto the sill, one leg inside, one leg outside.

I swung my leg over and tried to lower myself to the waiting room floor. It wasn't easy. I set my foot down on an end table covered with out-of-date children's magazines and it nearly tipped over. Luckily, I still had a firm grip on the windowsill, so I managed to keep myself from falling. I tried again, making sure I put my weight squarely at the center of the table, and made it to the floor safely.

The waiting room was so quiet that the soft gurgling of the fish tank filter practically sounded like a raging waterfall. Over its incessant gurgle, I could hear my own heartbeat, punctuated by anxious, quivery breaths.

The waiting room posters and pictures that had looked so annoyingly babyish in the daytime now had a sinister quality. As if Flopsy the Bunny were about to leap from the painting near the front door and sink its oversize rabbit teeth into my neck.

As I made my way toward the corridor leading to the examination rooms, I paused to look into the fish tank. Huh. I'd never noticed it before, but those little guys looked a lot like Mr. Googly Eyes, the pet fish I used to have before I accidentally sent him to fish heaven when I fed him a bit of one of Mom's cakes.

"Nice fishies," I said softly. "Just pretend I'm not here, okay?"

My eyes were probably playing tricks on me in the gloom, but it almost looked like they turned toward the sound of my voice.

I made my way down the hallway to the room where Dr. Shallix had taken me earlier. I slowly opened the door and stepped inside. There was no window in there, so it was nearly pitch-black. I strained my eyes but couldn't make out a thing. So I stooped down and started feeling for the garbage can.

After bumping my head against the leg of a desk (twice), I managed to find it. Reaching in and groping around for the phone, I came up empty. I even pulled the plastic liner out to see if Will's phone had somehow slipped underneath.

No luck.

I did find a rubber glove on the floor next to the trash can, though. Without thinking, I popped it in my mouth. *Chewy*. I rolled my eyes at myself in the dark. Why did I have to be so gross? I spat the glove out and tried to think where else I could look for the phone. It had to be somewhere.

Just then, I heard the front door of the office open and shut. And the hallway light clicked on, piercing the dark of the room with a painfully bright sliver of light.

CHAPTER 10.0:
\ < value= [I Go Dumpster Diving] \ >

MY HEART NEARLY BURST OUT OF MY
chest. For a long moment, I stood frozen with fear.
Then I snapped out of it and dove behind the end of
the exam table.

"There is no need to be afraid," a voice said from the
hallway. His voice.

At first I thought Dr. Shallix was talking to me. But
then he continued, "We will just have a little talk. You
like to talk, yes?"

I heard a scared, muffled whimper in response. It
sounded like a kid.

I squeezed myself into a tight little ball, wishing I

could become invisible. Or, better yet, disappear alto-gether. I looked around wildly, desperate to find a better place to hide, sure that in a few seconds Dr. Shallix would walk in and find me.

I started to sweat.

And suddenly I really had to pee.

I listened to two sets of footsteps shuffle down the hall. They got closer and closer. In a few seconds, I saw a shadow cross the doorway. They were coming in!

For a dozen excruciatingly long seconds, their shapes loomed in the doorway, not more than ten feet from me. Finally, I heard a set of keys jingle in a lock. The shadows moved and disappeared with the sound of a closing door.

I peeked around the exam table. The hallway was empty. My chest loosened and I took in a big gulp of air. I had to get out of there. Fast.

But even so, I hesitated. I didn't have what I had come for: Will's phone. I struggled to quiet the voice in my head that kept screaming *run away*, and resolved to keep looking.

I cautiously approached the door, then darted out into

the hallway, trotting on my tiptoes to avoid making a sound. Ducking into the first doorway on my left, I found myself in one of the other exam rooms. With the light still on in the hallway, I quickly located the garbage can and searched it. Empty. The same thing went for the can in the third room.

Will's phone wasn't anywhere.

I let out a deflated sigh and snuck back out to the waiting room. I didn't want to stick around any longer than I had to. I tried the front door, but it wouldn't budge. I looked up at the window and realized I'd have to go out the way I came in.

I climbed onto the blue vinyl couch next to the end table, and my sneakers let out a loud, plasticky squeak as they settled into the upholstery. I froze, on the verge of an all-out freak-out, waiting to see if Dr. Shallix had heard the sound. The door he'd disappeared behind didn't open. I inched over to the end table and carefully stepped onto it so I could reach the window.

Just then, I heard Dr. Shallix's voice in the hallway.

"You are comfortable, yes? Good, good. I will be right back."

My stomach plummeted like a satellite crashing through Earth's atmosphere. I grabbed onto the windowsill and leapt up from the end table. Unfortunately, the force of my jump tipped the end table onto one leg, where it balanced for several seconds. I didn't wait to see which way it was going to drop. I hoisted myself up to the window and started to lower my body down gently onto the Dumpster when . . .

CRASH!

The end table slammed to the floor, scattering magazines across the waiting room.

"Hello?" Dr. Shallix called out from somewhere inside. "Is somebody here?"

I let go of the windowsill and gravity took over. I tumbled headfirst into the Dumpster. A huge pile of garbage broke my fall.

I lay completely still, trying to blend into the trash. Something hard poked into my back, but I didn't dare shift position. I could barely breathe, which actually wasn't a bad thing, given the stench.

Still, that didn't stop me from fear-eating a used

tissue I found stuck to the side of the Dumpster.

"Hello?" Dr. Shallix called from the window directly above me, his teeth gleaming in the moon's cold glow. "Pumpkin, are you out there?"

Pumpkin? Who was Pumpkin? I hoped he didn't mean me, because Pumpkin was almost as bad as Trash-mouth.

"Pumpkin?" he said again. "Pumpkin?"

After a few seconds, the window slammed shut.

I counted to ten to make sure Dr. Shallix had really gone. The silence deepened. I reached around to move the thing that dug into my back. It felt kind of familiar. Smooth. Rectangular. Kinda . . . phone-like. I struggled upright to try to find a little more light.

It was a phone! With a screen that was spiderwebbed with cracks. Will's phone. Yes! I had found it!

My triumph lasted about three seconds.

I was rocked off my feet as the whole Dumpster jolted, propelled a good six feet farther into the alley by some huge . . . *thing* slamming into its side. Five hundred pounds of metal screeched on the pavement.

My hand hit the top edge of the Dumpster and the phone tumbled to the asphalt.

Something in the alley snarled viciously. It sounded a little like a dog, but much lower pitched. Like a cross between a wolf and a bear.

I scrambled up the pile of trash, desperate to find out what could be making that sound. Quivering, I grasped the smooth lip of the container and pulled myself up high enough to peek over the edge.

Right below me, with paws propped up on the side of the Dumpster and lethal-looking three-inch fangs dripping with saliva, was Pumpkin.

CHAPTER 11.0:
\ < value= [I'm Nearly Eaten by a Chihuahua] \ >

I KNEW IT WAS PUMPKIN BECAUSE IT
wore a pink-and-purple dog tag that said PUMPKIN.
Even in the dark, I had no trouble reading the tag—it
was roughly the size of a dinner plate.

The reason the tag was roughly the size of a dinner
plate was that Pumpkin was roughly the size of a pony.

Only Pumpkin wasn't a pony.

Pumpkin was a Chihuahua.

The largest Chihuahua I—or probably anyone else,
for that matter—had ever seen.

Pumpkin's massive dome-like head featured shiny
black eyes the size of bowling balls and ears practically

big enough to use as sleeping bags. It was like if you took thirty or forty Chihuahuas and mushed them all together to make one supersize Chihuahua.

As cute as that might sound, trust me, it wasn't. Mainly because Pumpkin seemed determined to eat me.

My mind struggled to understand what I was looking at. Maybe she'd chowed down on some radioactive waste along with her Alpo. Or maybe one of her parents had been an elephant.

Then she snapped at me, coming about an inch from tearing my face off, and any thoughts about why Pumpkin was so huge were instantly replaced by one overwhelming thought:

Aaaaaahhhhhhhhhhhhhhh!!!!!!!!

I dove back into the Dumpster. My heart thumped like a hyperactive hummingbird. For a few seconds, I heard nothing but silence. Then . . .

BOOM!

Pumpkin slammed her round head into the side of the Dumpster. The metal wall buckled.

BOOM!

The wall buckled some more. A few more head butts and she'd transform my stinky hiding place into a stinky coffin.

I pressed up against the rear of the Dumpster and tried to force my brain to stop freaking out long enough to think of something. How do you get rid of a three-hundred-pound Chihuahua? A fifty-pound strip of bacon? I wasn't about to find that in the Dumpster.

But I did find what felt and smelled like a half-eaten tuna sub. I took a little bite (I couldn't help it), and then I stood up and tossed it out into the alley, hoping it would distract Pumpkin long enough for me to make a run for it. Unfortunately, she snapped it out of the air and swallowed it in one bite.

I sat back down in the trash and tried to think of a way out. Even if climbing back into Dr. Shallix's office seemed like a good idea (which it didn't), the Dumpster had been pushed too far away. I couldn't reach the window.

I started to think there was no way out. And to top things off, I still had to pee. Bad. Really bad. I couldn't hold it much longer. I had to go. Like *now*!

At first, I figured I'd just go right in the Dumpster. I mean, it was already filled with nasty garbage, right? So who would notice? But being tossed around in a Dumpster of garbage and pee was too gross even for me. So I searched around until I found an empty milk carton and I . . . well, I used it.

When I finished, I threw the half-full carton out into the alley, where it hit the ground and tipped out its contents. I kind of felt bad for littering. But at the moment, littering was the least of my problems.

Suddenly, Pumpkin stopped growling at me. She sniffed the air, turned around three times, and headed straight for the puddle of pee.

Then she started rolling in it.

Eww!

Dogs can be so disgusting sometimes.

After a few seconds, I realized she was so interested in the puddle of pee that I might just be able to sneak out of the alley past her. I slowly eased myself out of the Dumpster until I stood on the ground. So far, so good.

I started out of the alley, but then I remembered the phone. Glancing back at Pumpkin to make sure she was still preoccupied, I tiptoed back to where the phone lay on the asphalt, picked it up, and put it in my pocket.

Yes! I had it! As soon as I got home I could—

Uh-oh.

Pumpkin spotted me.

She stood up and took a step in my direction.

I took a step backward.

Then she took another step toward me.

This continued until I backed right into the wall at the end of the alley. I was trapped. And Pumpkin, teeth bared, moved closer and closer.

When she was inches away from me, I closed my eyes and braced myself to be ripped apart.

The thing is, Pumpkin didn't rip me apart. Instead, she pressed her nose against my hand and sniffed. Then she let out a happy little yip, trotted back to the puddle, sniffed it, and then came back to smell my hand again. She cocked her head at me, reared up, and pinned me against the wall, licking my face all over.

Yuck! I guess she liked my pee.

After about ten seconds of subjecting me to her smelly dog breath, she stopped licking me and went back to rolling in the puddle. I figured that was my cue to leave.

When I finally made it home, my alarm clock told me it was 1:46 a.m. I had been gone less than two hours. But my whole body felt drained. It seemed more like two days. I could barely find the energy to untie my sneakers.

Once I kicked them off, I tucked Will's cell phone into the back of my sock drawer for safekeeping and flopped down on top of my bed fully dressed. A sense of hopelessness settled over me like a cold, wet blanket. Sure, I had found Will's broken phone. But I had also found yet another thing that made me doubt my own sanity—a three-hundred-pound Chihuahua. Who would believe me if I told them I'd nearly gotten chewed up by a lapdog big enough for the Statue of Liberty's lap? I wasn't completely sure I believed it myself.

Fortunately, within minutes, sleep pulled my eyelids closed, and all the disturbing thoughts bouncing around my brain were crowded out by a dream in which I lived in a house made out of cheese.

CHAPTER 12.0:

\ < value= [We Have Lunch . . . with a Side Order of Pain] \ >

THE NEXT MORNING I WAS WOKEN UP

extra early. By something stinky. Which, I realized a few seconds later, was me. I sat up in bed and looked at myself. Rancid garbage juice from the Dumpster covered my entire body. And my bed. My parents would kill me if they caught me like this. Luckily, judging by the loud snores that reverberated through the house, they were still asleep.

I got to my feet, stripped the bed down to the bare mattress, and threw the bedding, along with my dirty clothes, into the washing machine. After a quick shower, I hoped my parents would be none the wiser. Although finding that I had willingly washed my own sheets might make my mom suspicious. I'd have to take that chance.

By the time my parents woke up, I had already dressed, eaten breakfast, and gotten ready for school. I tucked Will's phone safely into my pocket and headed out early, eager to see if I could catch Will before home-room and try to get it working.

Will wasn't there, though. He didn't show up at school until halfway through social studies. He muttered something about a doctor's appointment to the teacher and sat down at the desk next to mine.

I was dying to talk to him about the phone, but our social studies teacher, Ms. Mahana, ruled with an iron fist. One word out of turn spelled detention. So I sat there, counting the seconds until the bell rang for lunch, feeling like I was going to explode with impatience.

When it finally did, Will and I loaded our trays up with food, made our way outside to the courtyard, and sat at our usual table away from everyone else. We liked to pretend we did this by choice, but the reality was, nobody wanted us sitting at their table.

As soon as we sat down, I started whispering. "Dude, where were you last night? I tried calling your house like a million times."

He shrugged. "Umm . . . my parents took me to have dinner at my aunt's. We got back late."

"Well, I need to talk to you about what happened Monday."

"Monday?" Will asked, shoveling a forkful of mac and cheese into his mouth.

"You know. My arm," I reminded him.

He shook his head and shrugged again.

I was getting annoyed. "Seriously, Will. I'm talking about my arm. It came off in your hand after I wiped out! Ring any bells? Something weird is going down!"

I stopped, suddenly aware that I was yelling. The last thing I needed was the whole school finding out that I thought my arm fell off. Even worse, Dr. Shallix made it painfully clear that I wasn't supposed to mention it to anyone. I took a deep breath and calmed myself down.

"All right," I continued, "then look at this." I slipped his broken cell phone out of my pocket and held it up.

"Yeah, so?" Will said flatly.

I looked around to make sure we were alone, then whispered, "It's your phone. It's proof that my arm fell off. You recorded the whole thing, remember?"

Will cocked his head. "Let me see that."

I handed him the phone. He pushed the power button.

Nothing happened.

He dropped it on the table. "Looks broken to me. Doesn't prove anything."

"Why are you being such a jerkwad?" I hissed. "You know what happened. You were there. I'm just trying to prove I'm not crazy, okay? And you're not helping. If we could just somehow watch the video on this phone, you'd see."

He stared at me for a moment, then went back to shoveling his food into his mouth.

I was just about to tell Will to stop being such a pain in the butt when I noticed something.

His lunch tray was empty.

It usually took Will every one of the twenty-five minutes we had for lunch period to finish his food. That's because he had to inspect every bite to make sure there weren't any earwigs in it. He never once actually found an earwig in his food. But his cousin had a friend who said he found an earwig in his food at a school just two towns over. For Will, that was close enough.

But there he sat with an empty tray. He'd simply chowed down on it without checking for a single earwig. And eating lunch like a normal kid was definitely abnormal for Will. I was just about to question him about that when I realized we were no longer alone.

"Hey," a voice said behind me.

Alicia Toth was standing next to the table.

Okay, a pretty girl talking to me two days in a row without using the words "trash" or "mouth"? Definitely weird. I mean, she had never said a single thing to me before yesterday in science.

"Hey," I echoed, trying to sound casual.

Will just looked at her.

She slid the backpack that she always carried off her shoulder and sat down next to me. "Mind if I sit?"

"No," I replied.

"Yes," Will said coldly.

"So I wanted to ask you about that thing with the electromagnet yesterday," she began. Then she noticed the smashed phone on the table. "Having phone trouble?"

"No," Will answered flatly.

"It's fine," I responded, picking up the phone and trying to put it back in my pocket.

She caught my wrist and deftly pried the device from my fingers. "I don't think this is fine. Looks all busted up to me."

While she spoke, Will just sat there glaring at her furiously. Like she was saying something nasty about him. Or had just kicked his puppy. It wasn't really like him.

"Can I have it back, please?" I asked, holding out my hand.

"Just a sec. I heard you say something about wanting to watch a video. Why don't you just take the memory card out and play it in something else?" She opened the back of the phone. "See? It's a micro SD card. You can use it with a ton of cell phones and computers."

She reached out to give me the memory card. But she never had the chance.

Because at that moment, Will sprang across the table and tackled Alicia to the ground. I looked down in horror at the tangle of flailing limbs that was Will and Alicia. Will actually looked like he was seriously trying to land some punches.

"Will!" I cried. "What are you doing? Get off her!"

Alicia yelped with surprise, then started fighting back. She had some serious moves. Like she was part ninja or something. She blocked a dozen of Will's punches, then clocked him with an elbow to the jaw. It sounded like someone smacking a side of beef with a baseball bat.

But if it hurt, Will didn't show it. He just kept punching.

I looked around the school yard to see if I could find a teacher or some students who could help me stop Will.

The grounds were empty. It was a cool, gray day, and everyone else had decided to eat inside.

In the meantime, Will stopped punching Alicia and wrapped his giant hands around her throat to strangle her instead.

Will was trying to kill her! Like, *really* kill her!

"Stop!" I screamed. "Will, stop!"

Alicia fought back ferociously. She punched Will, scratched his face, gouged at his eyes. When those things didn't work, she clawed around in the dirt until she found a rock about the size of an orange. She grabbed it and started smashing it into Will's face. But no matter how many times she hit him with it, Will wouldn't let go.

Alicia tried to suck air into her lungs, but with Will's hands around her throat, her effort was pointless.

If I didn't break this up, one of them—maybe both of them—would end up dead.

I sprinted toward them. I couldn't just stand there watching Will kill Alicia.

I took half a dozen steps.

Then I tripped over my own shoelaces.

After flying through the air, pinwheeling my arms and legs in a futile attempt to regain my balance, I slammed into Will just hard enough to break his hold on Alicia.

As I got unsteadily to my feet, I heard Alicia coughing and struggling to catch her breath. Good. She was alive.

I turned back toward Will just in time to see him scowl as he slammed me against the brick wall of the school. I felt like I had just been dropped from the top of a five-story building. It knocked the wind right out of me. *Man, when did he get so strong?*

"What are you doing? We're friends, dude!"

If he cared about the fact that we'd been best friends for almost our entire lives, it definitely didn't show on his face.

Wait! His face! It should look like raw hamburger meat. I saw Alicia totally mess him up with that rock. But I didn't see any kind of injury on his face. All I saw was rage. How could that be?

Will balled up his fist and brought it back over his shoulder, while holding the front of my shirt with his other hand. What the heck was going on?

"Will!" I cried as his fist started traveling toward my face. "What's hap—"

That's when Will's head exploded.

CHAPTER 13.0:
\ < value= [I See What's on Will's Mind [Literally]] \ >

THE SIGHT OF MY BEST FRIEND'S HEAD basically disappearing in a red mist was the most horrible thing I could ever imagine. Only I hadn't imagined it. It was real. As real as the solid ground that I hit with a *thump* when my legs gave way.

For a while, all I could hear was a ringing in my ears. The sort of thing you'd hear on Kill Squad III on Xbox if you set off a flash-bang too close to your character.

I saw Alicia walking over to me, with some kind of metal object in her hand, blood running freely from her nose and dripping from the tip of her chin.

She said something to me. At least, I saw her lips move, but I still only heard ringing.

She tried again.

"Get up!"

The ringing faded and the sounds of the school yard started coming back to me. The birds chirping. The wind rustling through the leaves. All as if nothing were different. As if my best friend weren't lying there motionless in the dirt.

"Did he hurt you?" Alicia said, extending her hand to me.

I took her hand, and she helped hoist me to my feet.

I shook my head. "Wh-wh-what . . . what happened? What's going on?"

I looked at the thing in her hand. A sort of hollow metal tube that she held by a handle. Her finger rested on a little lever that stuck out from the bottom. A trigger.

Rage boiled in my veins as I started to put the pieces together. "You killed Will!"

"Your friend wasn't a friend. He was a Tick." She didn't bother trying to hide the disgust in her voice.

"A Tick? What do you mean?" I questioned angrily. "You killed him!"

"Not him. *It*," she replied through clenched teeth. "And it got what it deserved."

Hot tears ran down my face. "He was my best friend. I've known him since first grade. And you . . . Why did you do this?"

She shook her head. "Because it needed to be done."

"Don't give me that!" I screamed. "You just blew up Will's head. Don't tell me you did it 'because it needed to be done'! What does that even mean?"

"Look at it," she said calmly. "Go ahead."

I closed my eyes and shook my head.

Her voice rose to a yell. "Do it!"

She put her hands on either side of my head and twisted until I faced what was left of Will.

"Open your eyes!" she snapped.

I swallowed hard and raised my eyes to where Will's head should have been. There, glinting in the watery light, was something square and metallic. A thick silver cable connected it to the rest of Will's body. I squinted at it. It looked like a . . .

"Central processor," Alicia informed me. "I told you, your friend was a Tick. If I hadn't done that, it would have killed both of us. And probably the rest of the school too."

My stomach flipped as I looked at the metallic device. I couldn't understand what I was seeing. "Wh-what's happening?" I croaked.

Alicia let go of my head and turned to walk away.

"What did you do to him?" I asked her. "What is that thing?"

She held up her weapon to show me. "This? It's an electromagnetic pulse gun. A *kleshch vzryvatel*. At least that's what we call it in Russian. I guess in English it'd be a . . . 'Tick popper.' It fires a small projectile that creates a really short, really intense electromagnetic pulse. Ticks hate it. You can probably tell why."

"Russian? Are you from—"

"*Nowhere!*" she barked suddenly, her voice so forceful I took a step back.

I stared at the gun. Was she going to kill me next? I lifted my eyes to meet hers. "Are you going to shoot me?"

Her face softened and she laughed humorlessly. "Not unless you're one of them. Don't worry. It wouldn't do much to a human anyway."

"Human? I don't understand. You're saying Will wasn't human? How can that be?"

She moved closer to me. "Look," she whispered. "You need to just put all this out of your head. Pretend you didn't see anything. Believe me, you don't want to know any of this stuff. Just go back to class and forget about it."

"But won't somebody find him? This?" I pointed to Will's motionless form.

"They'll make sure it's not discovered. The Ticks wouldn't want humans to know they're here. We need to leave. Now. Or we're dead. Come on."

She put her weapon away and turned to leave.

"Wait!" I pleaded. "What's going on? None of this is real, is it? I'm crazy, right?" Despite my best efforts to choke it off, a pathetic sob forced its way out of my throat.

I wiped my teary cheeks with the back of my hand.

Alicia stopped and faced me. She let out a long sigh. "Fine. I guess I owe you an explanation. Just don't blame me if it gives you nightmares so bad you wet your bed every night."

CHAPTER 14.0:

\ < value= [For the Record, I Don't Wet My Bed over This] \ >

ALICIA LEANED IN CLOSE AND SAID IN A tense whisper, "Sven, we're in trouble."

"Yeah, well, I guess going around blowing up people's heads would tend to get you in trouble," I replied angrily. "I can't believe you killed Will!"

She sighed. "Forget about Will. This is bigger than that. We're at war, Sven."

"What are you talking about? *Who's* at war?"

"We are. Humans. All of us. And the fight is going to decide the fate of the entire planet Earth. It's not like a regular war between countries. It's a war between species.

One of those species is human. The other, a synthetic life-form. Technological beings that have been manufactured, but are alive. These beings have the ability to think, to reproduce, to *live* just like any other life-form. Do you understand?"

And here I was worrying *I* was crazy.

What she said sounded laughable, but my gaze drifted back to that strange silver box protruding from the ruined flesh of the thing I'd always thought of as my best friend. "Are you talking about robots? Robots are trying to take over the world?"

"Not robots. The descendants of robots, I guess. They're cyborgs; part mechanical, part organic. They refer to themselves as Synthetics and formed an army to destroy humanity and create a new world that they control."

"Wait," I said. "You're saying there's some kind of huge robot war going on?" I paused to let the chirping birds make my point. "That's impossible. How come I've never heard anything about it? If it were true, it would be all over the news. . . ."

"Until now, the battle has been limited to a remote area in eastern Europe. Very few humans were even aware the Synthetic race existed. Just a few hundred humans in a secluded settlement. We call them 'Ticks.'"

Part of me wanted to run screaming from the insane girl with the deadly weapon. But part of me wanted to hear her out. "Hold on, if there were really some robots that wanted to take over the world, wouldn't pretty much every country get together and defeat them?"

"It's not that easy, Sven. But I should probably start from the beginning." Alicia tucked the Tick popper into her backpack and rubbed her eyes. "The former Soviet Ukrainian city of Chernobyl. You've heard of it?"

I nodded silently. We'd learned about Chernobyl in social studies. It was the site of a huge nuclear reactor meltdown. "So you're saying these . . . whatever you called them are some kind of radioactive mutants or something?"

Alicia laughed coldly. "Mutants? You've been watching too many movies. The nuclear power plant that melted down was part of a huge top secret Soviet laboratory complex that was built in 1962. It had advanced weapons labs, genetic modification facilities—and Laboratoriya 54u, an underground annex so secret that only a handful of the most senior Soviet officials even knew it existed. That's where scientists were working on robotics and artificial intelligence. And they were doing some really scary stuff. At least, that's what my parents told me."

She paused, cocking her head to the side, and stared at me. Like she was trying to see into my brain and figure out if I believed her.

But with Will lying dead in front on me, I wasn't exactly in the mood for a history lesson. "So how does this make it okay for you to kill my best friend?" I demanded angrily.

After a few seconds, she continued. "I'm getting to that. So by 1986, the scientists had created these thinking machines that were even smarter than humans. When the reactor exploded that year, the government evacuated the scientists, along with the entire population of the area, and created a thirty-kilometer exclusion zone.

There, the experiments they had been working on—the Synthetics—were left alone. Completely isolated. With no one to keep them from . . . evolving, creating more and more advanced versions of themselves until they were almost indistinguishable from organic beings. At first, we pretty much left each other alone. But a few years ago, they came to the conclusion that they, not humans, were adequately equipped to protect and manage Earth's environment and limited resources. That was when they started getting aggressive. Just a few attacks here and there at first. But eventually, it got worse."

Her eyes shone with tears and she turned away.

"Wait, so you're from—"

"Chernobyl," she said still facing away from me. "This war I'm talking about? It's been dragging on for years in Ukraine between Synthetics and a settlement of human holdouts who didn't acknowledge the exclusion zone around Chernobyl. That's where I'm from. I was born there. We were the only ones who knew of the Ticks' existence. But we couldn't say anything to the government. We were scared they'd evict us from our homes.

Or arrest us. Or . . . worse. So we fought the Ticks alone. Until . . ."

"Until what?" I asked.

She turned toward me, her mouth twisted into a pained grimace, tears streaming from her eyes. "All my people are gone. The Ticks wiped them out. And if the Ticks have their way, they'll do the same with the rest of the human population of Earth. They're already spreading, infiltrating cities, preparing for . . . something. I don't know what. But I'm the only one left who can stop them."

"So that's why you killed Will? He was—"

"*It*, not he," she hissed. "Will wasn't human. Look." She pointed to Will's body. "You see that?"

I forced myself to look at the figure laid out in the grass. His T-shirt had been torn in the struggle, and some sort of birthmark peeked out from behind the fabric. A red Ξ. "Yeah, it's a birthmark. So what?"

"It's not a birthmark, Sven. It's how Ticks designate different generations. This is a Xi model. An advanced one. Can't totally pass for human, but pretty close."

I shook my head. Something about what I saw was wrong. Something didn't fit. But *what*? Then it clicked. "Will didn't have a birthmark on his chest."

"What do you mean? You can see he did. It's right there," Alicia insisted.

I shrugged. "He didn't. His parents have a pool. I've gone swimming with him about a million times. I never saw that birthmark before."

"You're sure?"

"Positive," I told her.

Her lips pressed into a thin, pale line. "Has he been acting, I don't know . . . different lately?"

"Actually, yeah." I nodded. "For one thing, he's never been in a fight before. And he was just acting kind of weird today. I mean, he was always weird, but then he stopped acting weird. Which, for him, was definitely weird. He wasn't doing the sorts of things he normally did. You know, touching things. He had these little rituals. Stuff like that."

"Wait a minute. These changes only just happened? Then they must have replaced the real Will." She rubbed the back of her neck anxiously. "So that's not the only one. There have to be others who made the switch," she said quietly, with a hint of fear.

"Hold on, this Will is a fake?" I asked, a faint spark of hope flickering within my chest. "That means the real Will might still be alive, right?"

"Maybe," she replied grimly. "But it also means the rest of us might be dead."

Mom brought home a mushroom-and-onion pizza from Union Pizza House that night—my favorite. I ate three slices but didn't taste a bite of it.

I was too preoccupied trying to make sense of everything that had happened.

I didn't know what to believe anymore. A week ago, if someone told me we were in the middle of a war with some kind of artificial life-form, I would have grouped them in with the Bigfoot hunters and alien watchers and all those other conspiracy theorists. But with all the inexplicable things going on recently, who knew what was real anymore?

But what really consumed my thoughts was Will. Where was the real Will?

I bolted the rest of my dinner and mumbled good night to my parents through a mouthful of half-chewed pizza, then rushed to my room. I tried to call Will's house but kept getting sent right through to voice mail.

So I sat down in front of my desk and flipped open my laptop. I typed "Chernobyl robot war" into Google and scanned the search results. Mostly, they were just old news articles and Wikipedia entries on the nuclear reactor meltdown. Nothing useful.

But when I clicked on IMAGES, my legs went cold with fear. About halfway down the page, my eyes locked onto a dark, grainy black-and-white photograph that looked . . . familiar. It was a shot of a man holding up a metallic box attached to a thick cable. It looked just like Fake Will's central processor.

I swallowed down the lump in my throat and clicked through to the page the photo was from. It was a short article from an old newspaper called *Chernihiv Gazeta*.

The headline read: **Сумасшедший Говорит Роботы Живут Среди Нас.**

Great. It was in Russian. I copied part of the text from the article and pasted it into an online translator.

Crazy Says Robots Live Among Us.

Ivan Babikov, a resident of Chernobyl, said he found a dangerous race of the robots, which, he argues, escape a secret science lab. When hunting small game, he said, Babikov accidentally shot what he thought that it was a man. But when he examined the body, he found that it's part mechanical. Authorities transferred him to the Voronstova Siberian Hospital for the Criminally Insane, where he will remain until such time as he is determined not to be a threat to society. This is the eighth separate instance of the report of the robots that the *Chernihiv Gazette* has received this year.

No! I thought, trying to keep from hyperventilating as the meaning of what I read sank in. *How can this be?*

With trembling fingers, I clicked on the link in the article. Seven more articles from *Chernihiv Gazeta* loaded. I translated them all, one by one. The translations were awful, but they all told the same story. People were finding cyborgs in the woods around Chernobyl. And in each case, those people were sent to the Voronstova Siberian Hospital for the Criminally Insane as soon as they notified the authorities.

It was true! As much as I didn't want to believe it, Alicia was right!

I got up from my desk in a stupefied trance, kicked off my sneakers, and mindlessly licked their soles, swallowing down the fine grit that coated my tongue. Then I slid into bed. I lay there between the sheets, trying to convince myself that when I woke up in the morning, everything would be normal again. I was so tired I could barely keep my eyes open, but I still couldn't sleep because of the worries ricocheting around in my head.

Eventually, my eyelids closed and I fell into a restless sleep punctuated by dreams of faceless humanoid robots beating me with my own severed arm.

CHAPTER 15.0:
\ < value= [It's Not My Underwear] \ >

I WALKED TO SCHOOL THE NEXT MORNING
in a paranoid haze, viewing everyone I saw with
suspicion. Alicia said there were other Ticks already
here who'd taken the real Will and replaced him with
one of their own. Which meant they could be anywhere.
Anyone. Old Mrs. McKenzie from down the street
tottered by, walking Hambone, her blind Boston terrier.
Could she be one of them? Could Hambone? Or there!
That police officer. Did he just beep? Or was it his
walkie-talkie?

I tried to shake the thoughts from my head. They
were just people. Right?

"*Caw caw cuhkaw!*" squawked a crow that had landed on the telephone wire above me. "*Caw!*"

Another one fluttered down next to it.

"*Caw caw thircaw,*" it croaked. "*Thirteen!*"

What? That crow hadn't really just spoken, had it?

I stared up at it. It stared down at me.

"*Thirteen!*" it shrieked. "*Caw! Soak us slappy!*"

The patch of sky above me darkened in a flurry of beating wings as twenty more crows landed on the wire. It sagged under their weight. The air was filled with the shrill calls of the birds.

"*Caw! Soak us slappy! Soak us slappy! Thirteen! Caw! Caw! Cuhcaw! Soak us slappy!*"

Ice-cold dread chilled my veins. What was with these birds?

I sprinted to the corner and headed right, trying to put as much distance between myself and the crows as possible. Pain stabbed at my ankle as I stepped into a pothole and my foot rolled over. I crashed down hard and skidded to a stop, the asphalt etching a road rash into the palm of my left hand.

A fluttering sound in front of me prompted me to open one smarting eye. A crow had landed on the pavement inches from my face. On its head, a bouquet of bright white feathers stuck up like the bristles of a brush.

It stared at me with unblinking eyes. And then ...

"*H-h-happy birthday to you!*" it screeched. "*Happy birthday to you! H-h-happy birthday, dear Sven! Happy birthday to you! Thirteen! Soak us slappy! Soak us slappy! Ha-ha-ha-ha-ha!*"

I had no idea what was happening. And I didn't want to wait around to find out. I struggled to my feet and took off toward school, limping as fast as I could, the creepy bird still laughing behind me.

As soon as I got to school and pushed my way through the double glass doors, I started hearing snickers coming from pretty much everywhere. But with all the crazy thoughts of killer cyborgs and fake best friends jostling for space inside my head, I couldn't wrap my mind around what was supposed to be so funny.

That all changed once I reached my locker.

There, taped to my locker door, hung a piece of paper.

It took me a second to understand what I was looking at. But when I did, a block of lead formed in my stomach and the skin on the back of my neck prickled with embarrassment.

Someone had taped a picture of me with my pants around my ankles standing in front of a big group of girls wearing a pair of too-tight pink underwear emblazoned with the word **TRASHMOUTH**. Only it wasn't really me, of course. Whoever had hung the picture up had obviously Photoshopped my head onto someone else's pantsless body.

I quickly tore down the paper, crumpled it into a ball, and threw it into my locker. I sighed with relief. Maybe no one else had seen it, I thought, slamming my locker door shut.

But that was when I noticed that every locker, as far as I could see all the way down the hall, had its own copy of the image. Hundreds of lockers. Hundreds of copies of the forged picture.

It didn't take a genius to guess who was behind it all—Brandon Marks.

"We need to talk," hissed a voice in my ear.

I turned to see Alicia standing beside me.

And just when I thought I couldn't be any more mortified, I felt my face flush and burn with even more embarrassment.

But if she found the fake pictures of me funny, she didn't show it. Her face was serious. A hard light glinted in her eyes.

"L-l-listen," I spluttered. "These pictures aren't really me. They're fake. This never happened!"

"Well, I can fix that!" Brandon said behind me.

Instantly, my pants were yanked down to the floor.

"Ladies and gentlemen," Brandon bellowed, his mouth twisting into a cruel, crooked-toothed smile, "I give you Trashmouth Carter in all his glory! Let's give him a big round of applause, folks!"

As I stood there, wishing I could disappear from the face of the Earth altogether, the hundreds of kids who crowded the hallway before homeroom began to clap and whistle and laugh along with the bully. In a second, I was ringed in by the jeering faces of half the school.

I'm pretty sure nobody in the history of the world ever felt as bad as I did at that moment.

Alicia turned to Brandon. "Give us some space," she said in an icy voice.

"But the show ain't over yet." Brandon guffawed.

She flashed him a look that made the laughter die in his throat. A glare that radiated a dangerous, almost tangible threat. "I said get lost."

"Uh, well, whatever," Brandon replied uncertainly. "Later, loser." He sneered at me and dissolved into the crowd.

Within seconds, the rest of the kids took Brandon's lead and their laughter faded into silence. Soon, Alicia and I stood alone in the hallway.

I quickly pulled up my pants. "I—I—I . . . I'm— I'm . . ." I couldn't make any coherent words come out of my mouth.

For a moment, the hardness in Alicia's eyes seemed

to soften. "Kids can be jerks," she said quietly.

Then, in an instant, her gaze was cold and steely again. "We need to talk," she repeated. Grabbing my wrist, she led me through the empty cafeteria and outside to the courtyard. It was completely deserted. Everyone would be settling into their seats for homeroom by now.

She dragged me over to where Will's Synthetic copy had exploded the day before. Other than a little patch of trampled grass, there was no sign that anything unusual had happened.

"What's going on?" I asked as she stared at me in silence. She seemed jumpy and kept shifting her weight from foot to foot.

"I couldn't sleep last night," she told me.

I waited for her to say more, but she didn't. "Um, okay. Actually, I didn't sleep well either. Bad dreams."

She took a step closer to me. "You want to know why *I* couldn't sleep?"

"I guess. If you want to tell me." I had a bad feeling that I wasn't going to like the answer.

"Something was really bugging me. I just couldn't

stop thinking about what was on that memory card yesterday. What was so important that your Tick friend wanted to kill me over it? So I came back here last night with a flashlight and spent some time searching. It took a while, but I found it." She held up the memory card from Will's broken phone. "Know what's on here?"

My eyes widened. "Nothing. Just me wiping out on my bike. It's private. I can take that back." I snatched the card from her hand and started to walk away.

"You're one of them," she said quietly.

I froze.

"Turn around!"

I turned to face her.

She pointed the Tick popper right at my head. My knees gave out under me.

I looked up at Alicia from the grass. "What are you—"

"Shut up!" she barked, holding the weapon inches from my face. "I knew something wasn't right about you and that magnet in science class Tuesday. Now I have proof!"

I opened my mouth to say something, but no sound came out. I was too terrified to speak.

She yanked the sleeve of my T-shirt up, exposing my shoulder.

"You're a Tick!" she snarled.

"What are you talking about? I'm a kid," I pleaded, finding my voice. "I'm just a regular kid."

"Oh, yeah?" she sneered. "A regular kid, huh? Your arm came off and now you don't even have a scar. How do you explain that?"

"I . . . I can't explain it."

Alicia glared at me. "Well, I can. It was your emergency repair system kicking in. Which you have because *you're a Tick!*"

"Emergency repair system? I don't even know what you're talking about."

"Now stop pretending you're too dumb to understand me," she barked. "It's something all Ticks have to keep them from going into system failure when they're damaged. It's what healed your arm."

"But that doesn't make any sense." I held out my left

hand. The road rash from my earlier fall was raw and oozing. "Look! This didn't heal. How could I have this if I was a Tick? It's bleeding. It didn't get repaired by some emergency-whatever-you-called-it."

"That's because it only happens when you get messed up bad. Like losing an arm. A little boo-boo like that isn't bad enough to trigger it. Don't try to deny it. You and I both know you're just a filthy Tick!"

Could she be right? Was I a Tick? Memories of the incredibly bizarre events that had taken place over the last few days paraded through my mind—my arm coming off, my best friend being replaced, the talking crows, the electromagnet.

The truth of what she was saying detonated in my brain like a bomb, shattering any possibility of rational argument. Everything I thought I knew about myself was wrong. I wasn't a real person at all.

Yet the terror welling up from my stomach and my shallow, raspy breathing felt all too real. How could I be a Tick? How could this be happening to me?

I had no answers. But I had to say something or

Alicia was going to kill me right then and there.

"Wait! I can explain," I cried in desperation. "It was all just—"

"I don't want your explanations," she growled, staring down at me coldly as she pressed the Tick popper to my forehead. "I want your head."

CHAPTER 16.0:
\ < value= [I Want My Mommy] \ >

OKAY, I TOLD MYSELF. OKAY. BE COOL.

If you have to go out, at least go out with dignity. No sniveling. No begging. Just be like James Bond or Superman. Dignity, Sven. Dignity.

And that's when I started to cry. Or, to be more specific, I melted down into a pathetic puddle of tears, wails, and hysterical, high-pitched sobbing.

"I—I—I—I—" I stuttered. "I—I . . . Please don't kill me! Please! I'm not a bad kid! Please! I'm begging you, please! I want to go home!"

Through a blurry film of tears, I saw Alicia lower the gun just a bit.

"Stop that," she demanded. "Jeez, will you stop crying?"

"Okay," I bleated between snot-drenched eruptions.

"That's not stopping," she said. "That's crying more. And it's not going to help you. You're just like your friend I deactivated yesterday. You'd kill me the second you had the chance."

"That's—that's not true."

"Yeah, right," she snarled.

"You . . . you'd be dead," I said through my sobs.

"What?" she barked. "What are you talking about?"

"H-h-he was going to kill you. I saved your life. Why would I do that if I wanted to kill you?"

That probably wouldn't matter to her. But other than bawling like a baby, it was the only way I could think to get through to her.

She lowered the gun a little more and nodded. "Why did you do that?"

I wiped away a gob of snot with the back of my hand. "I couldn't just sit there and watch him kill you. I told you. I'm not a bad kid."

She squatted down next to me, studying my face. "What are you programmed to do?"

"Programmed? I—I don't know. Until two minutes ago, I didn't even know I was a ..." I couldn't bring myself to say it.

"Come on!" she snarled angrily. "Why are you here? Tell me!"

"I don't know!"

"Don't give me that!" Alicia roared. "You're lying! What are you doing here? What do they want you to do?"

I met her eyes. "Please. I don't know."

She stood up and kicked the grass in frustration. "Don't you lie to me! Tell me! Tell me about *srok rasplaty*!"

The breath caught in my throat. *Soak us slappy?* That's what the crows were saying!

"Wait! Did you just say 'soak us slappy'?" I asked.

Alicia sneered at me. "What? No. Don't be stupid. I said *srok rasplaty*."

"That's ... that's what the crows said," I gasped.

Her eyebrows shot up. "What crows?"

"The ones I saw on the way here this morning. There

118 **ROB VLOCK**

were a bunch of them. Following me and making these weird noises. They were saying 'soak' . . . 'sroak' . . . well, whatever you just said. And they kept saying 'thirteen.' And then there was this one that . . ."

I didn't want to tell her about the one that sang "Happy Birthday" to me. She'd think I was completely loony.

"There was this one that *what*?" she asked insistently. "Tell me!"

"Fine." I sighed, getting unsteadily to my feet. "You'll think I'm crazy, though. There was this one that sang 'Happy Birthday' to me. I swear it looked kind of like my pediatrician, Dr. Shallix."

"*Srok rasplaty*," she muttered. Then she sighed. "I'm sorry. I have to do this."

She raised the weapon again. I squeezed my eyes shut and held my breath, petrified with fear.

After several seconds, I still wasn't dead. I opened one eye a sliver.

The Tick popper shook in Alicia's hand. Then she abruptly lowered it.

"God, I suck at this!" she said through clenched teeth. "Ticks killed everyone I cared about. They took everything from me. And now I'm looking one right in the face and I can't pull the stupid trigger. Great."

"Please," I said. "I don't want to hurt anyone. Before yesterday, I'd never even been in a fight. Can't you just let me go?"

She shook her head. "You're too dangerous to have around. I have to deactivate you."

"Deactivate me? You mean kill me. It's killing, you know. I'm a twelve-year-old kid. A kid whose biggest worry up until two days ago was trying to somehow convince the population of Chester A. Arthur Middle School that I'm not the biggest loser in the world!"

"Stop talking!" Alicia snarled.

"I don't know how you think I'm dangerous to anyone," I continued, words flooding out of me in an uncontrollable torrent. "I'm just a big failure at everything I do! Everyone hates me! My dad thinks I'm a screwup! My mom thinks everything is just great because she's too oblivious to realize that her son has only had one friend in his whole life! And now you're here telling me I'm dangerous! The only thing I'm dangerous to is my own social life!"

"I said, shut up!"

My voice squelched into silence as I watched Alicia's finger tighten on the trigger.

CHAPTER 17.0:
\ < value= [We Could Get Suspended for This] \ >

A BUMBLEBEE BUZZED BY, AND FROM THE
school building I could hear the muted clamor of busy
hallways as my classmates continued their ordinary lives.

The muscles in Alicia's jaw clenched and unclenched
while she decided whether the Tick standing in front of
her should live or die.

Then something white fluttered between us in the
brisk morning breeze and came to rest in the grass at our
feet. It was a copy of Brandon's fake picture of me that
had probably blown loose from one of the picnic tables
outside. He may have been a big, stupid bully, but I had
to give Brandon credit for being thorough. Not only had

he plastered nearly every locker inside, but he had taped dozens of copies outside as well to make sure I couldn't escape my humiliation.

Alicia's eyes drifted down to the paper, and a hint of vulnerability flickered in her expression.

Finally, she let out a long sigh and lowered her weapon. She tucked the Tick popper away, and suddenly I could breathe again.

"What? Why . . . why didn't you . . ." I couldn't bring myself to say the words *kill me*.

"I know what it's like to be that kid, Sven. The one everyone hates." She closed her eyes and took a long, slow breath. "Besides, if I want to find out what's going on here, I might need to keep you in one piece. At least for now."

"But wait. It's not true, right? I'm not really a Tick, am—"

"Enough questions," she interrupted. "It's not safe here. We have to run."

I started off toward the cafeteria door, but Alicia put her hand on my shoulder and yanked me around.

"Not that way. We need to put as much distance as we can between us and the school. It's the first place they'll come." She paused to think for a moment. "Follow me."

I ran after her to the teachers' parking lot. Alicia darted through the first row of cars, trying each door as she passed. When she yanked on the handle of a blue SUV, the door swung open. She climbed inside.

"What are you doing?" I cried.

"Getting us out of here," she answered, ducking under the dashboard.

Ten seconds later, the engine turned over and the SUV started. How did she know how to hot-wire a car?

"Get in!" she ordered.

I hesitated. We couldn't just steal a car.

She revved the engine. "Get in the car or you're going to find yourself under it!"

I walked around the front of the car—pausing to lick some of the dead bugs off the grille—then climbed into the passenger's seat.

I looked out the window and my heart sank. A sign marking the parking spot read:

RESERVED FOR
PRINCIPAL PAPADOPOULOS

"Alicia, we're going to get suspended for this!" I complained.

She slammed the SUV into reverse, backed out of the spot, and shifted into drive.

"Better than getting dead," she replied as she stomped on the gas.

We zoomed out of the parking lot with a screech of tires.

We drove through downtown Schenectady without saying a word. I watched the scenery roll by and wondered how I was going to get out of this mess alive.

Eventually, Alicia broke the silence. "Those birds. Did they say anything else?"

I shook my head. "I don't think so. Just 'thirteen' and 'happy birthday' and '*srkoak*'—"

"*Srok rasplaty.*"

"Right. What does that mean, anyway?"

A worried look flitted across her face. "It's Russian. It means 'day of reckoning.'"

"That doesn't sound good. So what does it have to do with my birthday?" I asked, not sure I wanted to hear the answer.

She shrugged. "I don't know. Maybe *srok rasplaty* is going to happen on your birthday. When is it?"

"Two days from now. On Saturday."

"Then that's how long we have."

"To do what?" I asked.

"To find a way to stop the day of reckoning, whatever that is," was her reply.

"And . . . what if we can't?"

"Just ask your friend, Will, back there," she said, with an edge I found more than a little threatening.

"What happened to him? The real Will, I mean. Where is he? Is he . . . is he okay?"

Alicia toyed with her hair distractedly as she considered this. "I don't know. But they need the original to make copies. So there's a decent chance they're keeping the real Will alive somewhere."

"Then we have to find him," I said.

She stared at me. "We only have two days to stop *srok rasplaty*, and you want to take the time to find your little buddy?"

"Yes," I stated without hesitation. "He's my best friend."

Alicia shook her head slowly. "You're completely *bezumnyy*, you know that?"

I looked back at her blankly. "I'm . . . bezoom . . . bezz . . . what?"

She laughed. "You're crazy, Sven. Completely nuts."

I liked hearing her laugh. She might run around fighting cyborgs and hot-wiring cars, but her laugh was gentle and genuine. At the sound of it, the wall that stood between us seemed to crack just a little.

I couldn't help noticing how tightly she gripped the steering wheel, though. And that she kept checking the rearview mirror.

"So, where did you learn to steal cars and fight like that and stuff?" I ventured.

A shadow flitted across her face. "Where I come

from . . . it's a rough place. We all learn to fight. To fight the Ticks. To fight the government, if we have to. We get combat training in school, starting when we're six. Instead of gym. As for bypassing a car's ignition, I learned that in shop class."

"Seriously?" I asked. "They taught you to steal cars in school?"

She smiled slyly. "I didn't say they taught it to me. Let's just say it was independent study."

She steered us expertly toward the industrial part of town. Soon, modest single-family homes gave way to old boarded-up brick factories and warehouses covered in graffiti. Weeds and garbage lined the streets. This wasn't an area I'd want to wander around at night.

"Where are we going?" I asked.

"My place," she said. "You'll like it."

CHAPTER 18.0:

\ < value= [Alicia Has a Better Idea] \ >

I DIDN'T LIKE ALICIA'S PLACE. I GUESS I just had a thing against dark, damp places that smelled like wet dogs. Wet dogs that liked to roll around in really stinky cheese.

She lived in an old, run-down house set far back from a row of warehouses and industrial buildings. It had no electricity, no water, and only a few pieces of rotting furniture. It did have lots of rats, though. I watched a few of them scurry along the baseboards when Alicia lit some candles.

The shock of seeing the terrible conditions in which Alicia lived was quickly replaced by pity. And a sense of guilt. I had it so good compared to her. Sure, my house was pretty modest, but compared to this, it was a mansion.

"Um, this is . . . nice," I lied, smiling to mask what I really felt.

"No, it's not," she replied. "But it's out of the way. The nearest neighbor is a quarter of a mile away."

Hearing how far we were from other people suddenly made me feel isolated. Vulnerable. Without even realizing I was doing it, I tore a scrap of moldering wallpaper off the wall and stuffed it in my mouth.

"What are you doing?" Alicia asked slowly.

I swallowed down the pulpy mess I was chewing on. "What am I doing what?"

"You just *ate* my wallpaper!"

"Oh, did I? Yeah, I do that sometimes."

Alicia scratched her head. "You do what, exactly?"

"Oh, you know," I mumbled. "Eat stuff that most people don't think is edible. It's not, you know, a big deal."

Her eyebrows shot up. "Huh. I guess I always figured Brandon Marks called you Trashmouth because you said a lot of dirty words or something. But this . . . this is much weirder."

"Yeah, thanks for pointing that out. I try not to let people know I do it, for obvious reasons," I said. "I wish it was something I didn't do, but I can't help it. I guess it's just a glitch in my programming or something."

"Oh . . . right. A glitch." Alicia furrowed her brow and scratched her chin thoughtfully. "In your programming."

When she finished staring at me like I was a freak, she pried up a loose floorboard and pulled out four small white spheres that looked a lot like golf balls.

"Really? You hide your golf balls under the floor?" I asked incredulously. "Wow, you must really love golf."

"You definitely don't want to hit these guys with a golf club," she replied. "They're HE44A concussion grenades. They're from home. In case we need a little extra firepower."

I took a big step back.

She gently placed them in a pocket on the side of her backpack and zipped it up. "Relax. As long as they're disarmed, they're harmless." She gave me a sidelong glance. "Let's say I'll be responsible for holding on to them, okay?"

I immediately nodded.

"So," I said, taking in our run-down surroundings. "Is your mom home? Won't she be upset that you're not in school?"

She laughed grimly. "Yeah, right. My mom. No, I don't think she'll mind."

"What?" I asked, taken aback by the tone of her reply.

"I don't have a mom, Sven. Or a dad. I live here by myself."

"Wait, how can that be? I've seen you arrive at school in the morning with your mother."

"That's not my mom," she answered with a shake of her head.

"But I've *heard* you say, 'Bye, Mom,' to her when she drops you off," I protested.

Alicia rubbed the back of her neck and frowned at the floor. "Yeah, well, that's what I want people to think. But she's not my mother. Her name is Denise. I met her at the homeless shelter when I first got to town. She kind of took me under her wing. We help each other out. She's lonely. Doesn't have any family. So I spend time with her at the shelter. And she, in return, pretends to be my mother."

"Why? I don't get it."

"Because," she explained with a sigh, "what do you think would happen if any of the teachers at school found out I'm living alone here in an abandoned house that's overrun with rats? Child Protective Services wouldn't exactly be thrilled about that."

"Seriously?" I gasped. "You live here all alone?"

"Yeah. I'm"—her voice hitched—"I'm all alone." She wiped her eyes with the backs of her hands.

"And you can't go back home?"

Her eyes gleamed wetly in the glow of the candlelight. "There's nothing to go back to. Everyone's gone. Dead. The Ticks saw to that. Some of the scientists in the Settlement were able to download a few fragments of information from a deactivated Tick before its memory was wiped. They found out the Ticks were planning something called *srok rasplaty*. And that it was supposed to start in Schenectady. But that was all they got. No details about what *srok rasplaty* actually was or why Schenectady was so important. Somehow the Ticks must have known we were onto them. They wiped out the whole Settlement. Except me."

"Oh my God," I whispered. "How did you get away?"

Alicia's jaw clenched and she turned away. When she finally spoke, she ignored my question. "My mom is—*was* a linguist. She studied in the US. She loved it here. She's the one who taught me to speak English like a native. Ever since I can remember, she wanted our family to move here, and she didn't want me to stand out. She'd make me practice my American accent constantly. But my father . . . he felt like leaving would be betraying the Settlement. So we stayed. And now they're . . ."

A shuddering sob shook her frame. I put my hand on her shoulder to comfort her.

In a heartbeat, she slapped it away.

"What the heck?" she cried. "You do that again and you'll lose that hand, Tick!"

"Sorry, sorry," I stammered. "I just thought you were . . . Never mind. Sorry."

"I wasn't crying," she said defiantly, turning to face me with a hard glare. "Anyway, I was on my own, with no home to go back to. So I salvaged what I could from the weapons lab and figured I'd do my best to stop the day of reckoning. Which you and this Shallix guy seem to be right at the center of."

She stared at me, her eyes burning with a mixture of suspicion and contempt.

"Okay," I said, eager to change the topic. "So I should probably be heading home now."

"No," Alicia snapped. "I'm not letting you out of my sight. Not until we find out what you have to do with *srok rasplaty*. You're staying here."

A rat scurried over my foot. "No way! I'm not staying here!"

"Well." She shrugged. "You don't have to. I could just deactivate you now."

I chewed on my lip. Both options sucked.

"Fine. I'll stay. But I have to call my parents," I

insisted. "I have to let them know where I am so they won't worry."

"No way," Alicia responded immediately. "If anyone, *anyone*, finds out where you are, we're putting the whole world at risk."

"I can't just disappear. They'll freak!"

"They're just going to have to deal."

"Well," I snapped, "what do you think will happen if I don't let them know I'm okay? How long until they call the police? Every cop in New York State is going to be looking for me. How's that going to help us?"

She thought about this for a moment. "Okay, you have a point."

"So you'll let me call them?" I asked.

"Nope. I have a better idea."

CHAPTER 19.0:
\ < value= [Breaking and Entering [But Mostly Breaking]] \ >

"THIS IS NOT A BETTER IDEA. THIS IS A horrible idea," I said ten minutes later, as we parked Principal Papadopoulos's SUV a few doors down from Shallix Pediatrics. "We should be looking for Will."

Alicia ignored me.

"Just because you're ignoring me doesn't mean it's not a bad idea," I huffed.

She kept ignoring me until she turned off the ignition. Then she whispered, "It's a great idea, okay? Just take cover."

I got out of the SUV and slipped into the same alley

where I had first met Pumpkin. Luckily, the alley contained no giant animals at the moment.

I peeked around the corner and watched Alicia get out of the car with a bottle of drain cleaner we'd picked up at a convenience store on our way to Dr. Shallix's office. She walked around the bumper, opened the gas tank, and gingerly poured the drain cleaner in. Then she bolted into the alley, hands over her ears.

"How do you even know Dr. Shallix is a Tick?" I asked as we crouched, waiting for something to happen.

"Sven, you told me he has a three-hundred-pound pet Chihuahua," she snorted. "What do you think?"

"I guess you have a point," I replied. "He was always a little . . . off. Plus, he was awfully interested in keeping what happened to my arm a secret. So you're sure this is going to work?"

"Absolutely," she replied. "I read about it on the Internet. Drain cleaner plus gasoline equals *boom!* Perfect diversion. Any second now."

A whole bunch of seconds passed, but there was no *boom*.

Five minutes later, I dropped my hands from my ears and sighed. "This isn't working."

"You have a better idea?" she growled.

I thought for a moment. "Yeah, actually. Give me your phone."

Clutching her phone, I slunk along the wall to the front door of Dr. Shallix's office. His phone number was displayed in white letters right on the frosted glass door. I tapped the numbers into the phone and hurried back to the alley.

She looked at me. "What are you—"

"Shh!" I hissed.

Dr. Shallix's voice echoed through the handset.

"Hello? Dr. Shallix?" I said, trying to make my voice sound as deep as I could. "This is Officer Carter—uh, Cartersonman from the Schenectady Police Department. We have an unlicensed, uh, dog here that we believe belongs to you. Goes by the name of Pumpkin. We're going to need you to come down here right away to fill out some paperwork and claim her."

In the silence that followed, tendrils of fear wriggled

down the back of my neck. He wasn't buying it.

Finally, he spoke. "Of course, Officer. I shall come as soon as I am able, yes?"

"Very good, sir," I said. "We'll see you shortly."

Then I hung up the phone and handed it back to Alicia with a smug grin.

Alicia's eyebrows rose a fraction of an inch. "Yeah, not bad. But not as cool as my plan."

In a few seconds, Dr. Shallix emerged from the building. We peered around the corner and watched him lock the door and walk to his car.

Suddenly, he turned toward us. We dove back into the alley and pressed ourselves against the rough brick wall. *Did he see us?*

Alicia slid the Tick popper out of her backpack. We waited, expecting his big, bristly head to pop around the corner and discover us. But after a few seconds, the car door opened and closed. The engine started and Dr. Shallix drove off toward the police station.

We crept to the office door and pulled on it. It didn't budge.

"Locked. Great plan, Einstein. How are we going to get in?" she asked.

"Follow me," I said confidently, leading Alicia back into the alley.

The Dumpster that Pumpkin had damaged was gone. A new one stood right below the window.

"There," I said, pointing up at the window.

I took a step toward the Dumpster, when *SMASH!* Alicia hurled a chunk of concrete through the glass.

I turned on her. "Why did you do that?"

"That's how we're going to get in, isn't it?"

I climbed onto the Dumpster and easily slid the unlocked window open. Glass fragments rained down around me.

"Oh," Alicia said a little sheepishly. "I guess that works too."

I led Alicia through the waiting room, past the tank full of fish, and down the hall to the door Dr. Shallix went through the other night.

"I got it," Alicia said. She pulled a crowbar out of her backpack.

"Hold on," I said as she started to put the crowbar to the door frame. "Is your answer to everything to break it or blow it up?"

She nodded thoughtfully. "Pretty much." She placed the end of the crowbar between the door and the frame. She leaned into it, and with the sound of splintering wood, the door sprang open.

We stepped into a windowless, pitch-black room. "So, hey. I was thinking," Alicia said as we searched for a light switch, "isn't the police station only about four blocks from here?"

Oops. I hadn't thought of that.

"We have to hurry," I whispered.

"You think? Wow, that fancy computer brain of yours sure is smart," she replied.

I shot her a look that said her sarcasm wasn't appreciated. Of course, she couldn't see it in the dark.

I found a switch and flipped it. The room suddenly flooded with bright light. It was much larger than I'd expected. Big, metallic machines lined the walls, glinting beneath the cold fluorescent tubes. It looked more like some kind of super-high-tech laboratory than a pediatrician's office.

Alicia grinned. "Bingo."

She walked around, inspecting various pieces of equipment, occasionally pausing to run her fingers over a set of controls.

When she came to a massive machine with what looked like two sliding doors on the front, she stopped. The contraption stood about eight or nine feet high and probably twice as wide. In between the two doors were a cluster of impossibly complex-looking controls. Mostly touch screens with a few dials and buttons thrown in for good measure.

"Here it is." Alicia smiled.

I raised my eyebrows. "Here what is?"

She looked at me and smirked. "Your momma."

"Ha-ha," I replied sarcastically.

She cocked her head. "Who's joking? It's a replicator. Basically a big copy machine. It's what Ticks use to reproduce. I figured if Shallix made himself a big pet dog, he'd probably have one. It's a pretty cool piece of gear, actually. You can assemble a new Tick from design plans or make copies of existing Ticks or, well, just about anything that's alive. Humans, animals, whatever. It's what made you. Now get in."

"You're going to copy me?" I asked in alarm, suddenly feeling like her plan was even worse than I had suspected. "I guess this is the part of your plan you forgot to tell me."

"Forgot. Chose not to. Whatever. We need a copy of you to send home so your parents won't raise the alarm. I didn't want you to chicken out."

I didn't like where this was going. "Why would I chicken out?"

She shrugged.

"But wait. Are you sure this is a good—"

"Just shut up and get in the machine," she said, sliding her fingers across a couple of touch screens.

The door on the left slid open. But I couldn't get in. Because it was already occupied.

CHAPTER 20.0:
\ < value= [Will and a Half] \ >

"WILL!" I YELLED, RECOGNIZING THE TALL,
skinny form inside the machine.

His entire body, apart from his head, was tied up with a bunch of white bandages. I almost laughed, since it reminded me of the time he dressed as a mummy for Halloween a few years back using real bandages. Halfway through the night, he had to pee, but he hadn't left any way to get his costume off. In the end . . . well, let's just say it's a good thing that bandages are absorbent.

The look in Will's eye, however, immediately smothered any impulse I had to laugh.

"Help me! Get me out of here!" he cried.

I stepped over to untie him, but Alicia pushed me aside. She had her Tick popper pointed at Will's chest.

"What are you doing?" I exclaimed. "It's Will!"

"We don't know that," she said coldly. "We've already dealt with one Tick that looked like him."

"Alicia, put down the gun!" I yelled. "Help me untie him!"

"Not until we see what's behind door number two," she insisted.

With a few swipes of a touch pad, she made the second door slide open, revealing a huge glass cylinder filled with a bloodred liquid. The liquid started draining out of the cylinder. As soon as the last of the liquid was gone, the glass slid down into the floor.

And there, standing in the machine was . . . something. It looked kind of like . . . well, I couldn't tell what it looked kind of like, since I had never seen anything that looked like it. From the waist down, it was . . . Will. I could tell because of the skinny, freckly legs and huge feet. But from the waist up, it was just a small square metal box—a central processor—sticking up in the air on the end of a silver cable.

"What is *that*?" Will and I said together.

"An incomplete copy," Alicia told us. "Shallix must have started it just before we called him. Mom and Dad told me they saw something like this wandering around the woods once. If something interrupts the replication process, this is what you get."

She kicked at it halfheartedly. "Without the upper half, it's pretty much harmless."

Half Will took a few steps forward, bumped into the examination table in the center of the room, and fell over.

Alicia put the Tick popper away and helped me unwrap the real Will. It was like a really bizarre Christmas Day where Santa gave out goofy, skinny kids instead of toys. Still, I was pretty relieved to have my best friend back.

As we unwound the bandages, I turned to Alicia. "How did you know he'd be here?"

She looked at the floor for a moment before answering. "I didn't. I just came here to find a replicator. Honestly, I was kind of hoping you'd forget about Will so we could focus on, you know, stopping the day of reckoning."

"You seriously would have just left him?" I gasped. "How could you do that? How can you not care?"

"I didn't come here to save *him*. I came here to stop the Ticks. We only have two days, remember?"

"You know what? If everyone were like you, maybe the human race wouldn't be worth saving!"

She glared at me. "Oh, is that what you want? You're sounding more and more like the Tick you are!"

I fumed at her silently.

"Um, guys?" Will said in a daze. "What's going on?"

We filled him in. He looked a little sick when we got to the part about Fake Will's head exploding like a piñata full of raw meat. I thought it was a good analogy, anyway.

When we finished the story, Will nodded gravely.

"That . . . that . . . sort of explains a lot, actually," he said.

For his part, Will didn't have much to add. The night after my arm fell off, he woke up in the back of Dr. Shallix's car. He was brought here, tied up with gauze when he tried to escape, and stuffed into the replicator without any explanation. Other than bathroom and meal breaks, he'd spent most of the last two days in the machine.

I clapped his shoulder. "Seriously, bro, it's good to see you. I thought you were de—"

Alicia interrupted me by clearing her throat loudly.

"Yeah, before you guys start planning some kind of bro party or whatever, maybe we can, you know, focus. Shallix will be back any minute now."

And, with that, she shoved me into the replicator.

CHAPTER 21.0:
\ < value= [I Meet the Worst Thing Ever] \ >

THE DOOR SLID CLOSED WITH A WHOOSH, and the machine began to hum. A deep blue light filled the little compartment, and my whole body felt like it was vibrating. Not like riding over a bumpy road or anything, but like every cell in my body was doing its own little dance. I could even feel my hair buzzing.

After a few minutes, the vibrating stopped and the blue light faded away. The door opened to reveal Alicia and Will staring at me expectantly.

"That felt weird," I said.

Will nodded. "I know, right?"

Alicia glanced at a display on the machine and

shifted her weight from one foot to another, furrowing her brow. "I hope we have enough time."

I glanced at Half Will lying on the floor. "What if I . . . *it* comes out like that?"

"It won't," Alicia said. "I think it won't, anyway. Copying a Tick shouldn't take as long as copying a human. Not as much data conversion or something. We learned about it in science last year. The programming might not be perfect, though."

I raised my eyebrows. "What does that mean?"

"Well, the body will be finished, but it may not act exactly like you. Programming the processor and neural network takes time. That's why Will's copy wasn't perfect. It was rushed."

"Wait," I objected. "Don't we need perfect?"

Alicia sighed. "Hey, if you want to hang out here until Shallix drives the four blocks back from the police station, be my guest. But I'd prefer to continue living, thanks. So . . ."

She pushed a button on the replicator.

As the liquid drained out, I had a moment of panic.

What if the copy came out . . . without clothes? Alicia would see me naked! Even if technically it wasn't *me*, it was still kinda my private parts we were talking about.

I quickly covered Alicia's eyes with my hands. "Don't look!"

Big mistake.

I found myself flying through the air as her combat training kicked in. I landed hard on my back on the floor.

"Sorry," she shrugged. "Reflex."

Just then, the glass cylinder slid down. I looked up from the ground, expecting to see myself standing there butt naked.

But what I saw was far worse.

Yes, my copy was naked.

That was bad. But instead of having a butt where people were supposed to have butts, my copy had a second face.

My face.

That was so much worse.

"How's it goin'?" the face attached to my copy's head

said to us as Fake Me stepped out of the replicator.

"What's up, my peeps?" said Butt Face.

Head Face tried to turn around to look at Butt Face, but only managed to spin Fake Me around and around in a circle.

"How's it goin'?" Head Face kept saying to Butt Face.

"What's up, my peeps?" Butt Face kept replying to Head Face.

I stared at myself in horror. This was like some kind of nightmare.

"What did you do?" I cried to Alicia. "This is horrible! That's never going to pass as me! My parents will know it's not me in about two seconds! You wanna know how? Because they know I don't have a *face* where my *butt* should be!"

"They'll probably like this one better," she said with a smirk.

I looked to Will for support, but he was too busy howling with laughter. "I just . . . I just want to know," he gasped as he struggled to catch his breath, "how he . . . how he poops!"

"Look," Alicia said, trying as hard as she could to keep a straight face. "Once we dress him, nobody will know he has a face for a butt."

"Oh, really?" I asked skeptically. "So what are we going to dress him in?"

CHAPTER 22.0:

\ < value= [Knock, Knock. Who's There? Death.] \ >

A FEW MINUTES LATER, I CAME OUT OF
an exam room wearing one of Dr. Shallix's suits that
we'd found hanging in a closet. It was itchy and smelled
like old dude, plus it was so big on me that it looked like
someone had zapped me with a shrink ray.

Fake Me, on the other hand, stood there comfortably
dressed in *my* clothes.

Well, almost comfortably, anyway. Butt Face wasn't
all that happy with the arrangement. His muffled voice
erupted from beneath my jeans. "Hey, my peeps! I can't
see. Pull down our pants!"

Head Face seemed to control the arms, so, thankfully, the pants stayed up.

Once Will had a chance to flick the lights on and off forty-seven times, the four of us left the secret lab, made our way down the hallway, and walked into the waiting room. Will stopped short as we started for the window.

"What's up with them?" he said, pointing at the fish tank.

When we came in, the fish had been swimming around like normal fish. But now they were all pressed up against the side of the tank, staring at us with their fishy, unblinking little eyeballs. Not swimming or eating or doing any of the things you usually see fish doing. Just staring.

"This is bad," Alicia whispered.

"What's the big deal?" I asked. "They're fish."

"Not quite. They're what we call watchers. Synthetics that are basically just living closed-circuit security cameras. Usually the Ticks make them look like small animals. Birds, a lot of the time. Anyway, it means Shallix probably knows we're—"

A knock at the office door interrupted her. Through the frosted glass, we couldn't see what it was. But we could see its silhouette. Whatever it was, it was big. Like, fe-fi-fo-fum big.

"Um, we probably shouldn't answer the door, right?" Will whispered.

Before we had a chance to tell him how stupid that question was, the entrance to the office burst open with an explosion of shattered glass.

"Get back!" Alicia yelled.

She pulled out the Tick popper, but before she could use it, the single largest man I had ever seen walked in through the ruined door and swatted the weapon out of her hand. It hit the wall, ricocheted off, tumbled through the air, and fell with a *splash* into the fish tank.

Calling him a man, though, might have been a bit of a stretch. He looked more like a giant person-shaped sack of skin stuffed with softballs. His muscles bulged out all over the place, straining at the fabric of a suit that, I noticed, looked nearly identical to the one I wore. He was maybe seven feet tall and, like, a million pounds—all of it muscle. His arms looked about fifty percent longer than they should have been. They literally dragged on the floor when he walked.

The weirdest thing about him, though? The overall impression he gave was like an overgrown, deformed, seriously ripped version of Dr. Shallix. The same coarse white hair and shallow, unblinking eyes. Like a giant Mega-Shallix.

Will gaped at him wide-eyed. "Who—*what* is that?"

"It's a Tick. He's been modified for hand-to-hand combat." Alicia ducked under one of the guy's swinging arms and rolled to the side. "They start with a basic humanoid form, then improve it."

"Doesn't look like an improvement to me," Will whimpered, ducking behind a potted plant. He pulled the copy of me down with him and tried not to attract the Tick's attention. Then, as usual, he curled into the fetal position and stuck his fingers in his ears.

Alicia whipped a knife out of her backpack and pushed me out of the way just as the raging creature swung a massive arm at me. "Look out, Sven! Stay back!"

She slashed Mega-Shallix's arm. A long red gash opened up the length of his forearm, but it might as well have been a mosquito bite—he didn't even flinch.

Even though my brain was mostly preoccupied with trying to find a way to put as much distance as possible between myself and the killer Tick, I couldn't help but wonder why Alicia had saved me from him. I mean, I was the enemy, wasn't I?

When the big sack of muscle made a grab for Alicia, she rolled to the left and hacked at the back of his leg, just behind the knee. She leapt out of the way as his right knee buckled, then thrust the knife up under the monster's ribs. He dropped heavily, the floor shaking under his weight.

For a second, I thought she'd killed him.

But no such luck. As I watched, the wound on his forearm closed up like a zipper. The blood that stained his clothes seemed to get sucked back into his body. A second later, he stood on his feet, as good as new.

Mega-Shallix's massive hands reached out toward

Alicia's throat, but she ducked and avoided his grasp. She darted under his legs and popped up behind him, her knife plunging half a dozen times into his back before he had time to turn and face her. But he still didn't react. She might as well have been stabbing a side of beef.

She continued to dodge his attacks—rolling away when he tried to crush her with his size-twenty feet, knifing his arms whenever he reached for her.

But I could tell she was getting tired. And it wouldn't take more than one hit from this guy to break every bone in her body. I had to get her Tick popper.

Alicia slashed again at Mega-Shallix with her knife. He caught it in his bare hand and ripped it from her grasp. It whistled by my ear as he tossed it away, and stuck into the wall right between the eyes of a dancing teddy bear decal.

He grabbed her by the throat.

"No!" I screamed. "Let go of her, you ugly toilet-brush-headed freak!"

I took a deep breath and sprinted toward the fish

tank. I only made it two steps before the giant Synthetic slammed me against the wall. I struggled to catch my breath, pressed up against a flu vaccination poster by a body as wide as an eighteen-wheeler.

Mega-Shallix wasn't done with me yet. He let go of Alicia, who fell to the floor, gasping for breath, and wrapped his huge hand around my head. Then he started to squeeze. Everything turned red as the pressure in my eyeballs increased. Another second or two and my head was going to be goo.

"Sven!" I heard Alicia scream.

Through a red blur, I saw Alicia pull her knife out of the teddy bear's head and start frantically stabbing at Mega-Shallix. He barely even noticed.

Then Mega-Shallix spoke. It sounded just like the normal Dr. Shallix, only deeper and more distant. As if the real Dr. Shallix was talking to me from the bottom of a well. "Sven, I am very disappointed in you. Very disappointed. Come with me now to complete your mission, and I will release you. I will even promise to finish your friends off quickly."

This is it, I thought. *We're doomed.*

Without warning, the half-completed Synthetic copy of Will we had left on the floor of Dr. Shallix's lab came ambling into the waiting room from the hallway. It walked over to Mega-Shallix, bumped into his massive leg, stumbled backward, and fell against the side of the aquarium. The fish tank rocked back on its pedestal, then tipped forward onto the floor with a huge crash.

An explosion of glass. Fish flopping everywhere. The Tick popper skittered across the floor.

At least it had been enough to get Mega-Shallix's attention. He turned to see the source of the noise and stepped on a flopping Synthetic fish. His foot slipped out from under him, his legs flew up, and he landed heavily on his back on the floor.

Well, technically, it wasn't the floor he landed on. It was the Tick popper. There was a brief crackle of electricity, then—

WHOOOM!!!!

The Tick popper exploded. Along with Mega-Shallix.

His grip on my head loosened, and I realized that, apart from his arm, there was very little left. The Tick popper had reduced him to a big puddle of red, slimy . . . *yuck!*

I pried his fingers from my skull and rolled onto my back, gasping for breath. My head felt like somebody had been using it to drive nails.

"Is everyone okay?" Alicia called out.

Will and my copy got up from behind the potted plant. Will nodded, slack-jawed.

Alicia ran over to me. "Sven! Can you walk? We have to get out of here before Shallix sends something else!"

She helped me to my feet.

"Wait. So that wasn't actually him, right? Dr. Shallix?" I asked her. "He was . . . he was horrible!"

She shook her head. "He must have modified a copy of himself to guard the office. The fish probably alerted him."

She picked up the remains of her Tick popper. It had blown apart like a firecracker. "Man, we needed this," she said.

"Can you fix it?" Will asked.

She dropped it on the floor. "It's junk. The entire magazine must have exploded." She wiped her knife off on the leg of her pants, then put it away. "Whatever. We'll make do. Let's get out of here."

I stopped her. "Wait. Did you ever think that you could have just let that thing kill me and there'd be one less Tick in the world?"

I saw her jaw clench. "It occurred to me."

"So why didn't you?"

She glanced at the ceiling for a second or two. Then she turned toward the exit. "Let's go."

Alicia, Will, my copy, and I stepped over what remained of the front door and headed toward the principal's SUV.

"Hold on a second," I said to the others. "Alicia, what about the drain cleaner you put in the gas tank?"

She put her hands on her hips defiantly. "What? You want me to admit my plan didn't work? Is that it?"

"No," I countered. "It's just that it might not be—"

"Fine," she interrupted. "You want me to say it? I'll say it. My plan didn't—"

KAAAABOOOOOMMMMMM!

Heat singed our faces and shattered glass and twisted metal showered down around us as Principal Papado-poulos's SUV exploded into a massive fireball.

CHAPTER 23.0:
\ < value= [I Really Get to Know Myself] \ >

THE EXPLOSION LIFTED ALL FOUR OF US off our feet and threw us backward almost ten feet. We tumbled through the air and landed hard on the pavement. Well, *I* landed on the pavement. Everyone else landed on me. My face was wedged against Fake Me's backside. I could hear Butt Face's muffled voice through the seat of my jeans. "What's up, my peeps?"

"Is everyone okay?" Alicia asked, pulling me to my feet.

"I think I fell on my face," Fake Me replied.

The acrid smoke from the burning car made me cough. "What happened?"

"Hmm, delayed reaction, I guess," Alicia mused. "Maybe I should have added more drain cleaner."

"I think maybe we should discuss how much drain cleaner you should have added once we're out of here," Will suggested as the sound of sirens filled the air.

Once we made sure there were no serious injuries, we took off at a run in the direction of my house. It was a fair distance away, but with the principal's SUV lying in about a million pieces on the street, running was our only option. Unless we wanted to wait for another Mega-Shallix to show up.

We took off at a sprint, looking back over our shoulders every few seconds to make sure nothing was following us.

A few blocks away, we stopped to catch our breath.

"That was horrible," Will panted. He turned to Alicia, a look of admiration spreading across his face. "How did you fight him like that? Weren't you scared?"

"Me? Scared of that little thing? Nah." She tried to sound casual, but her voice shook when she said it.

When we were sure nothing was coming after us, we circled back toward my house.

On the way, I got to spend some quality time with myself. Which really sucked, because myself was a huge pain in the butt.

At first, Fake Me just stared at me for, like, two minutes straight as we walked, tripping and stumbling over the uneven sidewalk. Then he tried to pick my nose. I don't mean he tried to pick the copy of my nose on his face. He tried to pick *my* nose. The one I was breathing through. I swatted his hand away and turned my back toward him.

That wasn't much of an improvement, though, since he just kept poking me in the back and trying to stick his fingers in my ears.

"Stop it!" I yelled.

Fake Me stopped. For about three seconds. Then he started making fart noises with his armpits.

Alicia turned to me. "Sven, cut it out!"

"It's not me!" I cried. "It's him!"

"Looks like you to me," she replied.

Then she and Will snorted with laughter. Fake Me started laughing too, even though it was totally unfunny.

I glared at him. "Just stop being annoying, okay?"

He looked back at me, his eyes kind of crossing and uncrossing and crossing again.

He burped. Five times.

Then his finger found his own nose. He pulled out a big, green booger, studied it for a few moments, and sucked it off his finger with a *slurp*.

"What the heck?" I screamed. "What did you do, Alicia? I'm some kind of drooling, idiotic loser! This is never going to work. There's no way my parents are going to believe this is me."

"I told you the programming might not be quite right," she responded. "It was a rush job."

"Not quite right? This is a disaster!" Then I had a horrifying thought. "He's going to school in my place, isn't he? He's going to make my entire middle school career even worse than it already is! Everyone's going to think I'm a slobbering moron!"

"No comment," said Will. Then he held out his hand and Alicia slapped him five.

"You guys suck," I grumbled.

By the time we arrived at my house, I was about ready

to kill myself. By *myself*, I meant Fake Me. We stopped behind a row of bushes around the corner and spent a good half hour trying to teach Fake Me how to talk to my parents the right way. It didn't go well.

"Okay, repeat after me. Hi, Mom, I'm home," I said to my double.

For him, that translated to "How's it goin', Mom?"

Then Butt Face called out from inside Fake Me's pants, "Did you say something, my peeps?"

"I said, 'How's it goin', Mom?'" Head Face replied.

"What's up with that, my peeps? I'm not your mom," Butt Face pointed out.

"Look, can we try something else?" I asked when they had finished laughing. "How about, what's for dinner, Mom?"

"Hey, Mom. How's dinner goin'?" was his version.

"Dad, I spent two hours practicing throwing the football," I tried.

"Dad, how's the football goin'?" Fake Me said.

"Hey," Butt-Face chimed in, "what's up, my peeps? I can't see anything. Pull down our pants."

It was completely hopeless. But Alicia didn't really care if Fake Me totally destroyed my life while we were figuring out how to save the world. She just aimed him toward my house and told him good luck.

We watched Fake Me ring the front doorbell. My mom opened the door and hugged him. Then he tried to pick her nose. Then the door closed.

CHAPTER 24.0:

\ < value= [I'm Really Mean to a Woodland Creature] \ >

ONCE WE HAD SET FAKE ME LOOSE UPON
the world, we hurried back to Alicia's place.

"So, I'm just gonna head home, okay?" Will said nervously when we got there. He flipped the light switch on and off forty-seven times, even though the house had no electricity. "My parents are probably freaking right now."

"Do you really think that's a good idea?" Alicia said.

"Why wouldn't I think it's a good idea?" Will asked.

"No reason," she answered calmly. "Except Shallix

will be looking for you. Because you know he's actually an evil Tick and not a real human. But, you know what? Good for you for standing up to him."

She walked to the door and opened it for Will.

The color left Will's face and he started flipping the light switch again. "Um, you know, uh . . ."

"But if you want to hang out here for a while, that's cool too." Alicia grinned. "It's totally safe here."

As if on cue, we heard a scratching of claws on the wood floor and something darted into the room. All three of us jumped about a foot in the air. But once we got a good look at what had joined us, Will, Alicia, and I exchanged embarrassed glances. It was a squirrel.

Just a regular old squirrel.

Except for the white, spiky fur that stood out all over its oversize head.

Oh, and the fact that it talked.

"Ha-ha, I see you," it chuckled in a high-pitched chitter. "You thought you could hide, yes? But there is no hiding from me. I can find you wherever you go."

Will and I backed slowly away from the creepy

talking squirrel. But Alicia just stared at it with a half smile on her face.

"I take it you're Shallix?" She said "Shallix" like it was a swear word.

"Ah," the squirrel replied after running up to her and sniffing her feet. "You must be the girl from the Settlement. I am sorry I cannot meet you in person. This avatar lacks . . . dignity, yes? But it is an excellent form in which to follow a group of naughty children. Still, I am saddened that I will not have the chance to kill you face-to-face."

The squirrel laughed. It sounded like the real Dr. Shallix on helium.

Alicia wasn't impressed. "Oh, I'm so scared. So what are you going to do? Nibble me to death with your little squirrel teeth?"

"No, no," Shallix Squirrel answered. "I have created something very special for you—the two things that humans are most scared of. You will meet them shortly, yes? They are on their way here now."

The Shallix Squirrel turned to me. "And you, Sven.

It is good to see you are still functional. But why am I calling you that? I should call you by your real designation. *Seven*."

"What . . . what are you talking about?" I asked uncertainly. "What do you mean 'Seven'? My name is Sven."

Dr. Shallix chuckled. "No, no. That's what your human parents called you when they adopted you as an infant after I created you. They have no idea who you really are, of course. Your actual designation is Seven Omicron, yes? You are the seventh model of the Omicron line."

I shook my head. "Omicron line . . . ?"

"Of Synthetics. You should be proud of that. A perfect reproduction of a human being, yes? Not even a real human can tell the difference. Except for maybe a doctor. Which is why I am here. I replaced the human Dr. Manson Shallix well before you were fabricated to ensure your true nature would not be discovered. You have been functioning marvelously, by the way, yes? Right down to your fart subroutine and nose-picking algorithm. I oversaw that part of your programming myself," he added proudly.

"I don't pick my nose!" I objected.

"Of course you do. You have been programmed to act like an average human in nearly every way, yes? You are so very special, Seven. Our secret weapon, designed to carry out the ultimate offensive against their disgusting race. And on your thirteenth birthday, *srok resplaty*, you will be ready to destroy every repugnant human on Earth and win the war for us once and for all."

"What?" I cried. "No! I don't want to destroy anyone!"

Hearing him tell me that I would be responsible for destroying humans felt like someone had just punched me in the heart.

"Of course you do, my boy. It is why you were created." He scurried closer to me. "I can offer you one more chance, Seven. Come back with me and carry out your mission, yes?"

I stepped toward the rodent, feeling a surge of anger boil up from deep inside. "Come with you so I can help you kill humans? Your computer brain must be malfunctioning! Why would I ever come with you?"

"Why?" he asked with what probably would have passed for a smile if he hadn't been a squirrel. "That is a very good question, yes? Tell me, Seven, how have the human children treated you at school? With kindness? Acceptance? No. I have been watching you over the years. They hate you. They hate how you are different. That is one of the biggest shortcomings of the human race—they despise what does not fit into their preconceived notions of normal. You are superior to them all, Seven, yet for your whole life you have been shunned, shamed, bullied by humans. You are surrounded by humans, yet you are virtually alone, yes?"

His words were like a punch in the gut. Everything he said was true. It was as if he was reading my emotions straight from the inside of my heart. My stomach burned with . . . what? Anger? Shame? Hatred? Envy? Maybe a mixture of them all.

My throat tightened and my breath came in short, raspy gasps.

"But among Synthetics, Seven," he went on, "you will

be a hero. An entire race will owe you its gratitude. And you will be there to see it flourish in centuries to come. I can stop you from aging, Seven. I can give you eternal life."

"What are you talking about?" I breathed. The floor felt like it was tilting this way and that. My whole world threatened to turn upside down. "Eternal life? You're . . . you're nuts."

At the mention of nuts, Shallix Squirrel turned in a tight little circle and chattered excitedly. "Nuts! Where?" Then he recovered. "My apologies. This body sometimes has a mind of its own, yes? But I am not insane, if that is what you are suggesting. It can be done, Seven. The key is in your blood. Which, technically, is not blood at all, but a transport matrix made up of simple iron-carbon composite nanomachines. Each of these microscopic machines is capable of extracting raw materials at a molecular level from the food you eat. They use those building blocks to create living tissue, just like that of a human. That is how you could appear to grow from an infant into an adolescent boy—the transport matrix simply added to your body to perfectly mimic human aging. You understand, yes?"

I nodded, even though most of what he said sounded like science fiction.

"Good," he continued. "You see, I can program your body to sustain itself indefinitely, perpetually repairing itself. Eternal life, yes? Plus, I can make you stronger, taller, better-looking . . . whatever you like. I can make you a perfect specimen of humanity—if you will excuse the contradiction in terms."

"Sven," Alicia cried, "you're not listening to him, are you? People don't hate you."

"Well," Will corrected, "maybe not *hate* hate, but . . ."

Alicia glared at him. "You're not helping."

"But, but, I mean, they're just jerks," Will corrected sheepishly. "Anyway, *we* like you."

"Come with me, Seven," Shallix Squirrel squeaked. "You are still valuable to me. Your mission must be completed. I will give you the life you have always wanted, yes?"

"The life I always wanted?" I uttered. "Killing everyone on Earth isn't the life I always wanted."

"Please, Seven. Be reasonable." The words came out of the squirrel's mouth in a sickly sweet croon. "I would greatly prefer to keep you alive. Come with me. I can assure you it is far preferable to the gruesome death you and your friends will experience if you decline my offer."

"You're bluffing," Alicia snapped. "You won't kill Sven. He's your secret weapon. You need him."

Squirrel Shallix's fuzzy tail twitched convulsively. "Ah, but it is not a bluff. Seven, please understand, if the humans were to discover your true nature, you would never see the outside of a laboratory again. They would dissect you to learn your secrets. And if they were able to reverse engineer our technology, it could have far-reaching repercussions that would be . . . unthinkable. To stop that from happening, I would do anything. *Anything*. Even if it meant destroying our ultimate weapon."

Alicia shifted her weight uncertainly from foot to foot and stared at me like she was sizing up a math problem. An equation that would probably determine my chances of living through the afternoon.

Finally, she spoke. "Sven, don't listen to him. Don't

do it. Tell me you're not seriously thinking about going with him."

I swallowed hard and studied the dirty wood floors. A lot of what Dr. Shallix said hit too close to home. My whole life, I had been teased and bullied and excluded. And it felt awful. I thought about all the times everyone in my class but me got invitations to birthday parties. All the whispers behind my back. The pranks. The insults. The stares.

An image of an eight-year-old me materialized in my mind. Half of Mr. Akita's third-grade class surrounded me, laughing at me on the playground during recess. Each of them took turns pelting me with a red rubber kickball. The hollow, plastic **THUNK** of the ball smacking against my body still resonated in my memory.

What hurt worse than the ball, though, were the words they chanted in time with each throw.

Smelly Sven. Stupid Sven.

Mom's a goat and dad's a hen.

He looks like poop, he smells like butt.

He's ugly as a monkey's nut.

But now, everything was different. Yeah, I might have been the world's biggest loser, but I was a loser who had the whole planet's fate in my hands. I wondered what those kids from Mr. Akita's class would think if they realized how important I was to their very existence. What would Brandon Marks say if he knew? He'd probably think twice before calling me Trashmouth again.

I took another step toward Shallix Squirrel. "It's an interesting offer. I . . . I just have two questions for you, Dr. Shallix."

"Sven, no!" Alicia pleaded. "You can't do it!"

Will walked up to me. "Dude, come on."

I ignored them and stepped forward until I stood right in front of the furry gray animal that was trying to tempt me with immortality.

"Yes, my boy. Good," Shallix Squirrel said, rubbing its little hands together. "Now, what do you want to know?"

"First," I asked, "what exactly will I be doing in the mission you keep talking about? How will I defeat the humans?"

"I am afraid that would spoil the surprise, Seven.

But you will know it when it happens, yes? Simply think of it as my thirteenth birthday present to you. It will have to stay under wraps for a little while longer." He giggled, amused at the thought. "Now what is your second question?"

"I was just wondering," I asked. "Are you a flying squirrel?"

"What do—"

That was all he had a chance to get out before I swung my foot in a sweeping kick and sent him flying into the air and right through the glass windowpane.

CHAPTER 25.0:
\ < value= [I Change My Underwear] \ >

I HEARD A FAINT *SQUEAK* AS THE SQUIRREL
bounced off a tree a dozen yards away. I guess my dad had
it wrong. I should have practiced being a kicker, rather than
a quarterback. I felt kind of bad booting a squirrel through
a window, though. Even if he did totally deserve it.

"Nice kick." Will laughed, slapping me on the back.

Alicia was a little less enthusiastic. She just looked at
me with her eyebrows all scrunched up.

"What?" I asked.

"Nothing," she said dismissively.

I folded my arms over my chest. "You thought I was
going to go with him, didn't you?"

She shrugged.

"I'm going to take a wild stab here, Alicia, but I'm thinking you don't like me very much, do you?"

"So? I'm not particularly fond of my toaster, either."

"I'm not a toaster!" I countered, years of teasing forcing my anger to the surface.

She took a menacing step toward me. "You're a machine! A machine just like the ones that killed my parents! And you expect me to like you? I don't even know if I can trust you!"

That hurt. "What? You don't trust me? You really think I'd kill the entire human race?"

"You tell me! It's what you've been programmed for!"

"Look at me!" I yelled. "What do you think I'm going to do, gross people out by eating gross things until they die of grossed-outedness? Or do you think a bunch of nuclear missiles are just going to fly out of my butt?"

"I don't know what you're going to do," she said, suddenly quiet. "Eating gross things might be part of it, for all I know. If we could figure out what you're programmed to do, then maybe we could find a way to stop it that doesn't involve deactivating you."

"I wish you'd just call it what it is," I fumed. "Killing me!"

"Seems to me Shallix is the one who . . ." She trailed off, suspicion etched on her features.

"What? Why are you looking at me like that?"

"How did he find us here?" she asked pointedly. "How did he know where we were?"

"Maybe he's just really good at hide-and-seek," Will suggested.

Alicia frowned. "I don't think so. I think Sven led him to us!"

"No way!" I protested. "Why would I lead him to us? I have more reason than anyone to get away from him!"

"Maybe," she replied, scratching her chin thoughtfully. "Maybe . . . Hold on a second."

Alicia starting rummaging through her backpack intently. I hoped she wasn't looking for one of her grenades. But when she pulled out her hand, she was holding nothing more dangerous than a calculator.

"Hold this," she said to Will, thrusting the device into his hands.

Before either of us had a chance to ask what the heck she was doing, she used her knife to cut the cord off a broken table lamp. Then she darted out to another room and returned almost immediately with an old cordless phone handset.

I watched her curiously. "What are you—"

"Shut up," she interrupted. "I need to focus."

She grabbed the calculator back from Will and tossed it and the other two items onto a rotting side table. Her hands worked furiously, stripping the insulation from the cord, unbraiding the copper wire, and winding it around the antenna of the cordless phone.

"There," she said after finishing doing whatever she was doing.

"What is that?" Will asked, peering at the tangle of wire and electronic devices that Alicia held in her hands.

"Kind of a bug detector," she answered. "My dad showed me how to make one. Watch. Sven, come here."

I walked over to her cautiously. "What are you going to do with that?"

"Be quiet," she ordered.

Alicia pressed talk on the phone handset and began slowly waving it in front of my body.

Static hissed softly from the phone's earpiece as the contraption made its way over my head, my neck, and my shoulders, and down along my spine.

Suddenly, it emitted a loud *squawk*.

"What's that?" I asked nervously, trying to look back over my shoulder at where she was holding the device.

"That's how he found us. You have some kind of tracker installed. It's broadcasting a signal. That's what this detector is picking up."

"A tracker?" I cried. "Oh, no!"

Her lips compressed into a tight slit. "At least we found it. Which means we have options."

"What options?" I asked, not sure I wanted to know the answer.

"Well, I could remove it."

"No! No way!" I barked.

"Or we can block its signal," she continued.

I nodded vigorously. "Definitely option B!"

"Okay." She disappeared into the kitchen and came back a few moments later. "Here."

I caught the roll of aluminum foil she tossed to me. "What? You want me to wear an aluminum foil hat? Seriously?"

"No," she replied. "Not a hat."

"Well, then where . . ."

I followed her gaze downward until it rested somewhere between my thighs and my belly button.

So the thing about wearing a pair of underwear made out of aluminum foil is that it's uncomfortable. And sweaty. And kind of crinkly in all the wrong places. It was even worse than Dr. Shallix's suit.

Alicia waved her bug detector over my body. Nothing but static.

"It's working," she remarked with a smile.

"It sucks!" I moaned. "Feels like I'm wearing the Tin Man's diaper."

"Dude," Will chuckled. "I don't think the Tin Man wore a diaper."

"Whatever! It's awful!" I caught Alicia stifling a laugh. "You think it's funny?"

"Because it is," was her reply.

"You try wearing a pair of underwear made out of metal and see how you like it," I raged. "It's not funny, you big—"

"Uh, guys?" Will interrupted. "Did you just hear something?"

CHAPTER 26.0:
\ < value= [It's So Funny I Forgot to Laugh] \ >

WE STOPPED AND LISTENED. AT FIRST, all we heard was nothing. But then a laugh echoed through the empty house. A second one joined in. In a few seconds, a chorus of chortling voices shattered the silence.

"So, um, I take it those are the two things humans are most scared of?" I asked, nervously recalling Dr. Shallix's earlier threat.

My mind flooded with images of horrible things—laughing tigers, laughing grizzly bears, laughing dudes with machine guns, laughing Bigfoots. (Or was it laughing Bigfeet?)

"Come on, guys! Combat formation!" Alicia barked, sliding her knife out of her backpack.

I looked at her cluelessly. "Um, what exactly does that mean?"

In the meantime, Will balled his huge hands into fists and twisted his body into some kind of martial arts pose. "Like this?"

"You guys are hopeless! Just get in the center of the room with our backs facing each other. That way, nothing can sneak up on us," Alicia explained. "The first person to see anything, call out."

We did what she said.

For half a dozen seconds, we stood there listening to the sinister laughter. Then I saw a shadow move. The others did too, because at the same instant, they started yelling, as well.

"Over there!" I called.

"There's something!" Will shrieked, pointing at the window.

"At the south entrance!" Alicia shouted.

I didn't know which way was south. But it didn't

really matter, since we were being attacked from every direction.

"I think we're surrounded!" I cried. I looked around for some way to escape the room, but there was movement at every door and window. We were trapped.

Finally, something came into view.

It was . . .

What the heck was it?

It took a few seconds for me to register what I was seeing. Dr. Shallix had said he was sending the two things humans feared most. What he didn't mention was that he had combined them into one creature. Something so hideous, it made me want to barf.

What I had seen slither into the room was, from the neck down, a giant snake. At least ten feet long and as thick as my dad's leg. That was bad enough. But from the neck up, it was even more horrifying.

It studied us for a moment, yellow slit-pupil eyes peering out from beneath a curly rainbow wig. A round red nose and oversize polka-dot bow tie completed the picture.

A CLOWN!

"Join me, my brothersssss," it hissed.

An instant later, nine more creatures identical to the first, each with thick white makeup and painted-on fake clown tears, wriggled into the room.

Alicia wasted no time. She immediately attacked, slashing and stabbing at anything within reach.

The clown snakes sprang into action as well, lashing out with tails that ended in sharp, jagged spikes—like overgrown bee stingers glistening with venom.

Alicia swung her knife in a big arc and cut off two of the snakes' tails.

"Losers," she sneered at them. "What are you going to do now?"

The snakes answered by opening their red-ringed mouths far wider than any human could and angrily flicking out three-foot-long forked tongues.

One of the snakes lunged at me, and its tongue— covered with octopus-like suckers that had pointed spines sticking out of their centers—just barely grazed my cheek. And suddenly, my whole head felt like it was on fire.

"Arrghhh!" I howled, holding my head in both hands.

Alicia called over to me in midstab, "Sven, what's wrong?"

"The tongues," I groaned. "Watch the tongues."

Before I finished speaking, Alicia leapt into motion, spinning and jumping and jabbing with her knife even more frantically.

Within seconds, tongues and tails and clown heads littered the floor.

She stopped, out of breath, and panted, "That wasn't so bad."

The clown snakes didn't seem to like being cut into pieces, though. The various parts on the floor wriggled and slithered, rejoining the bodies they belonged to. In a few seconds, all ten clown snakes looked as good as new. They circled around us.

Suddenly, Will cried out, "Wait! Salt! Salt is deadly to snakes! All we need to do is sprinkle some salt on them! Alicia, where do you keep the salt?"

"Will," Alicia pointed out, "that's slugs you're think-ing of. Not snakes."

Will looked deflated. "Oh. Right."

Each clown snake raised its tail and aimed it toward us. Ten lethal stingers poised to strike.

We were dead.

Alicia slowly reached around and unzipped the side pocket of her backpack. She slid her hand inside and groped for something.

"No, you don't," a clown snake hissed. "Bad girl."

It uncoiled its body and drove its head right into Alicia. The impact sent her sailing through the air and into the far wall. She slid, unconscious, to the floor.

I looked at Will. His lower lip trembled and all the color drained out of his face.

Alicia moaned faintly but didn't move.

They don't deserve this, I thought through the pain that enveloped my head like a cloud of acid. *It's my fault they're in this mess. I need to fix it.*

"Wait!" I took a step closer to the deadly spikes. A drop of venom beaded at the end of the snake tail nearest me and dripped to the floor. It sizzled on the worn wooden boards. "I'll . . . I'll go back to Dr. Shallix. Just let them go."

"Sven, no!" Will cried.

I turned to him. "I have to do this," I said.

"Veeery goood," one of the clown snakes wheezed. "I will take you to our masssster, Dr. Shallixsssss. The others will sssssstay here to keep your friendssssss company."

"Okay," I said quietly. "But . . . I want to say good-bye to my friends first. Please."

The clown snakes looked at one another, and then the one that had spoken nodded.

I walked over to where Alicia lay on the floor and grasped her shoulders. Her head sagged to one side as I propped her up against the wall. A tear glistened on her pale cheek.

"Is that you, Mom?" she mumbled, still completely out of it.

I reached into her backpack and fished around until my hand closed on something round. A grenade! I pulled it out and shielded it from the clown snakes' view. I didn't want to use it—in a space this small, it would probably blow us all up. But maybe it could buy us some time.

I wheeled on the Ticks and held the grenade up

over my head so they could see it. "Okay, back off or I'll use this!"

A confused look passed from one clown head to another as they eyed me. One of them started laughing. Then another. All ten clown snakes quaked in creepy, high-pitched giggles.

"You think this is a joke?" I shouted as threateningly as I could manage.

"Um, Sven?" Will said shyly. "That's an apple."

I looked up at my hand. I was holding a small apple. Darn. I must have reached into the wrong part of Alicia's backpack.

The leader of the clown snakes slithered over to me, skewered the apple with its tongue, and swallowed it without even chewing. Then it wrapped itself around me and hissed in my ear: "Let'sssss vissssssit our friend Dr. Shallixsssss."

CHAPTER 27.0:
\ < value= [We Redecorate Alicia's Place [Not in a Good Way]] \ >

I FOUND MYSELF BEING SHOVED TOWARD
the living room door without so much as an apple to
defend myself with. As I was dragged past the table in
the center of the room, I looked around frantically for
something I could use as a weapon. All I saw was the
lighter Alicia had used to light the candles when we
came in. I grabbed it.

The clown snake paused when we neared the door and
called out to Will and Alicia, "Hey, kidsssss, time to diiiiiiie."

If you ever decide to become a clown, I recommend
that you stay far away from open flames.

Because as soon as I touched the lighter to the rainbow wig of the clown snake that was dragging me to the door, it erupted into flame. Its laugh was replaced by a deafening, agonized shriek. It let go of me, reared up, and tried to shake the fire out. But all it succeeded in doing was setting the rainbow wig of the clown snake next to it on fire as well.

Before I knew it, nearly every one of the monsters was screeching, trying to extinguish the burning wigs on their heads. And the smell! Let's just say it kind of reminded me of the time my dad singed all his hair off trying to get the grill going using a whole can of lighter fluid.

As the creatures writhed and slithered around the room, their flaming heads darting this way and that, they started setting other things on fire—tattered curtains, peeling wallpaper, a threadbare rug. If we stayed there much longer, we were going to get cooked.

The clown snakes scattered, suddenly far more concerned with extinguishing themselves than killing us. This was our chance. We had a clear path to the door.

At least, if you didn't count the smoke and flames now engulfing almost every part of the room.

Alicia struggled to her feet. Will and I each supported one of her arms and we took off at a run, shielding our faces against the searing heat as best we could.

We were almost out of the room when the lone clown snake who wasn't on fire slithered into our path. We moved to the right, but it lashed out with its tail and stopped us in our tracks. We darted to the left, but its head and deadly tongue were waiting for us.

It smiled at us and croaked, "Leaving so sssssoooooon? Why not ssssssstay awhiiiiile? We can all buuuuurn together."

We looked around for another way out.

There wasn't one.

Will let out a feeble whimper. But then something happened that I had never seen before. His whimper grew in volume and pitch until it became a bellow of rage.

"Let us out!" Will screamed. "Get out of our way, you clown school dropout!"

"And iffffff I don't?" the monster countered.

Will deflated like a punctured balloon. "I'll . . . I'll . . . make you?"

The clown snake laughed hysterically. "Sssssuch defianccccccce! Perhaps I'll eat you firsssssst!"

It slithered toward Will.

Stupid move.

As the creature slid by me, licking its lips hungrily, I flicked the lighter that was still in my hand. Instantly, its rainbow wig ignited in a fiery halo. It shrieked and writhed frantically, adding one more voice to the symphony of agonized clown wails.

We sprinted down the hall and emerged into the cool, fresh afternoon air, stopping under a huge maple tree, where we caught our breath.

"Will!" I said when I had regained the ability to speak. "That was brilliant!"

He turned to me with a dazed expression on his face. "What was?"

"The way you stood up to that stupid clown thing and distracted it so I could burn its ugly clown head," I told him.

He shook his head in confusion. "I did?"

Then his knees gave out and he collapsed to the ground in a dead faint.

Flames licked from the empty window frames, blackened the walls, and consumed the roof of the house. The screams of the clown snakes inside rapidly faded into silence.

We had escaped.

I smiled and turned to Alicia.

But she wasn't there.

I was just quick enough to spot her disappearing through the front door of the burning building.

"Alicia!" I screamed after her. "Alicia, stop!"

But she didn't stop. In a moment, her form was completely obscured by smoke and flame.

Despite every sensible impulse, I sprinted to the burning house and dove through the doorway after her.

"Alicia!" I shouted. If there was an answer, it was drowned out by the angry roar of the fire burning all around me. "Alicia!"

The hallway behind me collapsed in an avalanche of

flaming wood. There was no going back, I realized with a sudden rush of horror.

I pushed forward, trying to shield my face from the searing heat.

I called her name until my voice, scorched by the thick, black smoke, contracted into a strangled cough, but I heard no response.

By the time I made it into the kitchen, I felt like my lungs had shriveled into dried-out scraps of leather.

I couldn't breathe.

Blackness closed in on my vision, and I was vaguely aware of my consciousness being torn from me as I fell in a heap to the floor.

CHAPTER 28.0:
\ < value= [We Are the Schmidts] \ >

SOMETHING WAS SHAKING ME.

I opened my smoke-ravaged eyes and squinted up at the silhouette of a gangly form looming above me.

Will's voice assailed my ears. "He's alive," he screamed. "Alicia, he's alive!"

"He's also a moron," she snapped, pushing Will away and grabbing me by the shirt. "What the heck is wrong with you?"

"What?" I asked. Confusion clouded my brain like the smoke billowing overhead. "Alicia? What's happening?"

She yanked me into a sitting position and gestured

over her shoulder toward the blazing ruins of her house.

"That's what's happening! You ran into the building like a big, dumb, brainless Tick!" she snarled. "I barely managed to drag you out the back door! Why would you do something so stupid! Why did you do that? You're such an idiot!"

"Alicia," I croaked through parched vocal cords. "I . . . I . . ."

"You what?" she hissed through clenched teeth. "Tell me, Sven. You what?"

"I . . . I went in there for you."

She let go of my shirt and gawked at me. "You . . . you went in there for . . . *me*?" she asked in almost a whisper.

I nodded and broke into a fresh fit of coughing.

"Such an idiot," she said, the anger in her words belied by the tremor in her voice. "You are *such* an idiot, Sven Carter."

Pulling a bottle of water out of her backpack, Alicia pressed it into my hand.

"Why did *you* go in there?" I demanded once I had taken a few sips of water.

"Money," she replied bluntly, any hint of concern that might have surfaced from behind her cool façade evaporating in a flash. "I had some stashed in the dining room. Figured we could use it."

For the second time that afternoon, fire trucks wailed in the distance. They were quickly drowned out by a low, angry-sounding growl.

"Sorry," Will said, reddening with embarrassment. "That was my stomach. You guys got anything to eat? All I've had to eat over the past couple of days were some gross gray squares that Dr. Shallix gave me when he let me out of that machine."

Alicia nodded toward what was left of her house. "I had some stuff in there, but it's probably a little too well done by now. We need to find someplace to stay."

"Where?" Will asked. "We can't go home. He knows where we live."

"Don't worry," I said. "I have the perfect place in mind."

"This place?" Alicia sneered as we stood outside the Manor House Inn, Schenectady's biggest and fanciest hotel. "I can't even think of how many things are wrong with this idea."

"Well, thinking never was your strong suit," I snapped. "Listen, this is probably the safest place in town to be right now."

"Really?" she asked skeptically. "How do you figure that?"

I rolled my eyes. "What's the last thing Dr. Shallix would want right now? To be discovered. What do you think would happen if he sent a bunch of snakes with clown heads after us here? Or a giant Mega-Shallix? Half the city would see them. There's no way he'd let that happen."

"Fine," she admitted. "That makes some sense. You're not as dumb as you look, Sven."

"Actually," Will interjected, "um, he might be. This place probably costs, like, five hundred bucks a night."

"Relax, Alicia got money out of her house." I turned to her. "So, how much do you have?"

She dug around in her pocket for a moment, then pulled out a fistful of dollar bills and coins. "Let's see," she said, counting them up. "Twelve dollars and fifty-eight cents."

"You ran into a burning building for twelve bucks?" I asked. "Let me guess: Money didn't exist in the Settlement, did it?"

Alicia sneered at me. "Of course it did. We just didn't have much of it, that's all."

And I suddenly felt like a real jerk. "Sorry," I said quietly.

Alicia shrugged, then scratched her chin thoughtfully. "Listen, I think I have a way. Just follow my lead, okay?"

We walked into lobby of the hotel and took a seat on an overstuffed leather couch that smelled like furniture polish. Alicia kept her eyes glued to the front desk. After about fifteen minutes, a roundish middle-aged couple dressed in Hawaiian shirts approached the concierge.

Alicia jumped to her feet. "Stay here," she whispered.

"Hallo," the Hawaiian-shirted man said with a thick

German accent. "My wife und I would like to check out of room two fifty-four."

The concierge typed something into her computer. "Ah yes, Mr. and Mrs. Schmidt. I hope you had a pleasant stay?"

"*Ja, ja, sehr gut!* Very good," the Hawaiian-shirted woman said.

That was when Alicia sprang into action.

I watched in dismay as she scooped up an expensive-looking vase filled with cut flowers from a side table and lobbed it through the air toward Will and me.

We only had time to exchange wide-eyed gasps before there was an explosion of ceramic, water, and flowers at our feet.

The entire lobby went silent. Every eye in the place was on us.

Which, evidently, was what Alicia was shooting for.

While everyone was staring at us, she slid one of the couple's key cards off the desk and slipped it into her pocket. Then she slunk away toward the elevator.

We met her in front of the elevators. But only after

we spent several minutes apologizing to the angry concierge and promising we'd go straight to our parents, who she assumed were staying at the hotel, and ask them to punish us for destroying hotel property.

Room 254 was a heck of a lot nicer than Alicia's place. In fact, it was probably the fanciest room I'd ever been in. It had two huge king-size beds, a giant bathroom with a big hot tub right in the middle of it, and a balcony with a breathtaking view of downtown Schenectady. Well, as breathtaking a view as Schenectady had to offer, anyway, which was pretty much just some old buildings across the street.

"Nice room," I said to Alicia. "There's only one problem. Those people just checked out of it. As soon as housekeeping comes to clean it, they'll realize we're not supposed to be here."

She grinned at me. "I thought of that already. Watch and learn."

She picked up the phone and dialed the front desk.

"*Ja, ja,*" she said in a totally lame-sounding fake

German accent. "This is Mrs. Schmidt in room two fifty-four. We liked our visiting to your beautiful hotel so much, we change our mind und are wanting to stay another few days. You can please charge it to the credit card we have given you, *ja*?"

She listened for a few seconds, then, "*Ja, sehr gut. Dunkin' shines.*" She hung up the phone and looked at me like a smug know-it-all. "And that is how you do it."

She took off her backpack and placed it on a desk along the wall. Soon, the rhythmic scritching of metal filled the room as Alicia methodically honed her knife with a small sharpening steel.

Will threw himself down on one of the beds, picked up the TV remote, and started channel surfing.

And I slumped down heavily in an armchair, the energy leaving my body in a flood the moment my brain sensed we were temporarily safe.

I sat quietly, lost in my own head, thoughts of Shallix Squirrel's offer to turn me into some kind of immortal Super Sven ricocheting around the walls of my skull. I couldn't help but wonder why he had made me such a loser in the first place. If my mission had always been to kill all humans, surely Dr. Shallix and his Tick overlords could have come up with something better than a weird, trash-eating kid.

On the bright side, though, at least I wasn't as weird as Fake Me.

At the thought of my bizarro Tick stand-in, a frigid sense of dread fell descended over me. When Mom and Dad figured out Fake Me wasn't really me, what would they do? And what kind of disaster would be waiting for me back at school after days of having a jabbering idiot stand in for me?

It drove me crazy to think about, so while Will and Alicia argued about what to watch on the hotel TV, I picked up the cordless phone from the desk and slipped into the bathroom with it.

I dialed my number.

A few rings later, someone answered.

"How's it goin'?" a voice that sounded exactly like me said.

I sighed. "Hi, can I speak to Mom, please?"

"Who is this?" Fake Me asked.

"It's me. Sven."

"I'm Sven," Fake Me argued. "Who is this?"

"The real Sven," I spat.

"Who?"

"Me. The kid who you're a copy of."

There was a long pause, then Fake Me said, "Oh, the *other* Sven."

"What's up, my peeps?" I heard a muffled voice on the other end of the line say. "Who's on the phone?"

"No one," Fake Me said. "It's just weird Sven."

"Weird Sven? *I'm* weird Sven?" I asked angrily. "You're the one with the face where your butt should be!"

"Say, 'What's up, my peeps' from me," Butt Face mumbled.

"He says, 'What's up, my peeps?'" Fake Me told me.

"Listen, I need to talk to—"

"Hey," he interrupted. "Guess what I'm gonna do at school tomorrow."

Cold fear pulsed through my body. *"What?"*

"I'll tell you what. I'm entering the talent show, that's what."

"No! No, please tell me you're not going to . . . What are you going to do . . . You don't have any talent!"

"Speak for yourself," Fake Me said. "Butt Face and I worked out this really funny ventriloquism routine. See, I start a knock-knock joke, then Butt Face finishes it. It's hilarious!"

I couldn't stand to hear any more. Just the thought of Fake Me humiliating me in front of the whole school by telling knock-knock jokes with his butt made my stomach clench up like a wad of crumpled tissues. "Noooooo!"

A second later, the bathroom door burst open.

Alicia rushed in, knife in hand. "What's wrong?" When she saw me standing there with the phone, she scowled. "Who are you calling?"

"Um, no one," I lied.

A tiny voice called out, "How's it goin'?" from the earpiece. I hung up.

"You called your house, didn't you?" Alicia growled. "What is wrong with you? You're going to get us all killed!"

She was probably right. I shouldn't have made that call. But I wasn't about to give her the satisfaction.

"What's the big deal?" I asked with a shrug. "It was just a phone call."

Alicia shook her head grimly. "Now that we've blocked his tracker, Shallix is going to look for other ways to get to us. Maybe a watcher at your house. Or maybe he's tapped your parents' phone. You ever think of that? Now we have to assume he knows exactly where we are and will send some Ticks after us. This is about the *worst* thing you could have done!"

I stared at her. "Don't you think you're overreacting just a tiny bit?"

She gripped her knife more tightly. "Are you willing to bet your life that I am?"

We stared at each other until I finally broke the standoff, pushed past her, and wilted back into my chair.

I clenched my teeth angrily. I didn't know who I was madder at, Alicia or myself. She was being kind of a jerk. But she was also kind of right. Which meant I was kind of wrong. I mentally kicked myself for being so stupid.

But it wasn't like I was *trying* to let Dr. Shallix know where we were. She should understand that. I just wanted to talk to my mom. Let her know I was okay. I mean, there was nothing so terrible about that, was there? I was trying to be a good son. I didn't want her to worry. That was what good kids did, right?

Or was it? Maybe I wasn't being a dutiful son. Maybe I was being a dutiful Tick. What if everything I did really was just because of my programming and there was no real me at all, just a collection of 1s and 0s that determined every single thing I did? Every single thing I thought?

I looked down to find my fingers drumming tensely against the arm of the chair.

Am I a person?

Or am I just a machine?

Will's stomach let out a long rumble of complaint, breaking me out of my thoughts.

"I'm starving," he complained. "Can we go out to get something to eat?"

"No," Alicia snapped instantly. "It's not safe."

"But what's the point of hiding out if we're only going to starve to death?" he argued. "I need food."

"Fine," Alicia snorted. "Fine."

She snatched up the phone, jabbed at a button, and cleared her throat. "Hallo, this is Mrs. Schmidt in room two fifty-four. We would like to be eating three pepperoni pizzas. Please have room service send them up right away. *Ja, ja.* Good-bye."

She slammed the phone down. "Happy?"

None of us was.

As we waited in awkward, angry silence for room service to arrive, my fingers again started drumming against the chair.

They stilled when a knock rattled the door in its frame.

Knock, knock, knock.

Alicia positioned herself behind the bathroom door, where she could get a jump on anyone coming into the room.

"Relax," I said. "It's just our food. Probably."

"I'm not taking any chances. Answer it," she hissed, glowering at me.

Her reaction kindled a spark of anxiety in my chest. I took a few deep breaths. Blood pounded in my ears as I slowly moved to the door and turned the handle. Gritting my teeth and bracing myself for the worst, I pulled the door open.

There, in the corridor right outside our room, was . . .

CHAPTER 29.0:
\ < value= [A Meal to Remember] \ >

. . . OUR DINNER.

A metal room service cart covered with a crisp white tablecloth stood in the hallway. On top were three plates with shiny metal covers.

I let out a long breath, and the tension loosened in my shoulders. It was just our dinner.

"Good, I'm starving," Will said, wheeling the cart into our room.

I lifted the cover from one of the plates. But what I revealed wasn't a pepperoni pizza. It was a whole roast chicken. "Huh. They must have gotten the order mixed up."

I pulled the covers from the other two plates. Two more roast chickens.

"This sucks," Will complained. "I want pizza." He was already looking for the room service button on the phone. "We should get them to fix our order. I hate—"

He froze.

"What's wrong?" Alicia asked, sitting bolt upright on the bed, where she had stretched out.

Will's eyes were wide. "Th-that chicken just moved."

"Dude, you're totally craz—"

But he was right. One of the chickens was actually moving. It wiggled its little drumsticks like it was trying to escape from the plate and avoid being eaten. The other two chickens started to do the same.

"I—I'm not hungry anymore," Will stammered.

The three chickens struggled to their . . . well, they struggled to where their feet would have been if they still had feet. They stood up on their bony little drumsticks and unfolded their wings. But these wings weren't tasty little morsels glazed with buffalo sauce.

No, these wings grew as they unfolded, telescoping

until they were almost the length of my arm. They were muscular and powerful, each ending in a lethal-looking, three-inch talon.

For roast chickens, they were surprisingly agile. In unison, they leapt from the tray and launched themselves toward Will, Alicia, and me, their pointy talons slashing the air, seeking to sink themselves into our bodies.

Will scrambled across the room, his eyes trained on the sanctuary of the closet. He launched himself inside and pulled the door shut, a razor-sharp claw splitting the air where his face had been just a millisecond before.

Enraged, his chicken threw itself at the closet door, sending splinters flying as it punched holes in the polished wood.

"I don't even like chicken!" Will screamed from inside the closet.

Alicia ducked as one of the monstrous chickens lashed out at her with a vicious swing. Brandishing her knife, she hacked at the nearest wing, managing to sever it from the rest of the carcass.

But even losing a wing didn't deter the fiendish piece

of poultry. It swooped low, then launched itself at her again. With a quick lunge, she buried her knife up to the hilt in chicken breast.

Sparks shot out of the chicken with an electric crackle, and the smell of burning poultry filled the room. The dead bird slid off Alicia's knife and fell with a dull *thud* to the floor. It didn't move.

"Sven!" Alicia yelled. "They're Ticks! Go for the center of the chest! The CPU's in the chest!"

A talon arced toward my eye. I twisted away from it, the rush of wind left in its wake ruffling my hair. "Go for the chest? With what?" I cried.

I held up my empty hands to make my point.

"Here," Alicia called, tossing her knife to me.

The weapon sailed end over end toward me. I reached out to grab it.

And I caught it.

By the blade.

Aaarrgghhh!

I yanked my hand back and the knife seemed to fall in slow motion, tumbling toward my shoe until it stopped.

In my shoe. Point first.

I was actually glad that Fake Me was wearing my regular shoes. I had a pair of Dr. Shallix's ugly tan suede ones on, and they were way too big for me. The point of the knife narrowly missed my big toe and sank into the sole, sticking out of the top of my shoe, handle up.

If my chicken had had a face, I think it would have been laughing at me. It shook with amusement for a moment, then propelled itself off the blue-and-gray carpet, did a single flip in the air, and punched its talon right through my shoulder, pinning me painfully to the wall behind me.

I wrenched at the wing that had impaled my shoulder, but it was stuck too deeply into the wall. I was trapped. The chicken's free wing arced straight for my head. I raised my left arm just in time to catch the other talon in the meat of my forearm.

More pain.

"Help!" I called to Alicia.

But she had problems of her own. Will's chicken, having given up on getting into the closet, turned toward her and launched itself at her head.

Without her knife, all she could do was punch and claw at the bird. That may have helped tenderize the meat, but it didn't do anything to stop the creature from trying to kill her.

She needed her knife. It was still sticking out of my shoe, but I couldn't reach it with my shoulder pinned to the wall.

So I flipped the knife to Alicia with my foot. Only it didn't really work out that way. Sure, the blade slid out of my shoe when I kicked forward. But instead of sailing in a graceful arc over to Alicia's waiting hand, it went straight up and stuck into the ceiling.

"Dude, why the heck did you do that?" Alicia screamed at me.

"Sorry," I grunted, wrestling with the homicidal roast chicken. "I was trying to give it to you."

"Well, you didn't," she responded angrily.

I rolled my eyes. "Thanks for pointing that out."

My eyes stung as my chicken drew its sharp claw from the muscle of my forearm, dripping a trail of my blood on the carpet. The searing pain almost rivaled the pain in my shoulder where the other talon still had me stapled to the wall.

Waves of agony pulsed through my body. The only thought in my head was that if I didn't get away fast, I was done for. But the thing had refocused on trying to embed its free talon in my face.

My eyeballs rolled back in my head as I dodged weakly. The murderous entrée was readying to deliver its death blow.

Even then, as I was fighting the piece of poultry that was trying to end my life, my stupid compulsion kicked in. I flicked my tongue out and licked the chicken. It tasted . . . well, like chicken.

Then something unexpected happened.

Well, I mean, something *other* than being attacked by a trio of roast chickens. The knife that I had kicked into the ceiling suddenly dropped free, tipped over until it was point down, and buried itself up to the hilt in the lethal fowl.

A crackle. Burned chicken smoke. And my roast chicken dropped dead to the floor.

Alicia writhed on the carpet, wrestling with the last remaining chicken. Glistening with melted chicken fat, the thing was so slippery that every time she got hold of a wing, the chicken would wrench it out of her grasp and attack her with it again.

I retrieved the knife from the chicken at my feet, took a step forward, and plunged it into Alicia's foe. Like the others, it sizzled, burned, and dropped.

Alicia got up and kicked it across the room. It hit the closet door with a *thud*. Will whimpered from inside.

"It's okay," I called to him. "We got them."

One eye appeared as the closet door opened an inch. Will surveyed the room—once he saw for himself that all three chickens had been vanquished, he stepped out.

"That was . . . weird," he said feebly, then collapsed into a chair.

CHAPTER 30.0:
\ < value= [I Freak Myself Out] \ >

I STAGGERED INTO THE BATHROOM TO see what kind of damage the chicken had done. I was a mess. Blood trickled freely out of the hole in my shoulder. The deep gash in my forearm gaped and seeped. My hand throbbed and burned where Alicia's knife had cut it open.

Just as I was about to run out to grab the phone and call 911, the damaged tissue on my shoulder prickled with a strange tingling sensation. Like ants crawling all over the area. As I watched, the wound started to close in on itself and went from bloody to scarred to completely healed within a minute or two.

It must have been what Alicia was talking about—my

emergency repair system kicking in. Just like what happened when I wiped out on my bike.

I expected my hand and forearm to heal as well, but they simply kept dripping blood and stinging with persistent pain.

A gentle knocking sounded at the door.

"Come in," I called as I let the blood from my hand drip into the sink.

The door swung open and Alicia stepped in. "Are you okay, Sven? It looked like that chicken got you pretty good."

I held up my hand in reply.

"Nice." She smiled grimly. "I have bandages. Let me grab them."

She stepped out of the bathroom, then reentered a few seconds later holding a clean white bandage roll.

"Is there anything you don't have in that backpack?" I asked.

"Yeah, another Tick popper. That would be helpful." She wet a towel and began cleaning the blood from my right hand and left forearm.

I winced in pain.

"Sorry, almost done," she said gently, holding my gaze with an intense, green-eyed stare.

"What?" I asked once I started feeling a little uncomfortable.

She turned away and reached for the bandage. "Nothing."

"It had to be something," I pressed. "You were looking at me like I had two heads."

"It's just that . . . I don't know . . . you're different."

My shoulders sagged. "Yeah, 'different.' That's one word for it. Most kids just call me 'weirdo' or 'freak.' But 'different' is a little nicer."

"That's not what I mean," she responded. "I mean you're different from any of the Ticks . . . sorry, *Synthetics* I've seen before."

"Different how? Like I don't have the body of a snake and a clown nose and a rainbow wig?"

The corners of her lips pulled up into the hint of a smile. "Yes, that, too. But what I really mean is you're actually kind of . . . I mean, I kind of . . . well, you're the first one I don't want to introduce to the business end of a Tick popper."

I blushed. It wasn't that she'd said anything mushy or whatever. But it was still the nicest thing a girl had ever said to me.

She tied off the bandage on my arm and quickly wrapped my hand. "There you go. Did you get hit anywhere else?"

I gestured to my shoulder. "This one healed itself."

"I guess your CPU must have considered that one too major to leave unrepaired." She gently touched the hole in my shirt with her finger. "Jeez, a few inches to the right and it would have hit your recirculator."

"My what?"

"Your recirculator. It's what Ticks have instead of hearts."

"Do I need that?"

"Yeah." She laughed. "You need your heart."

"Well, then I'm lucky it wasn't a few inches to the right," I said, putting my hand on my chest.

"Yeah . . . lucky." Her smile was replaced by a look of uncertainty.

"What? What's wrong?"

"Nothing. Nothing's wrong," she replied in a carefree voice. But the way she bit her lip made it pretty obvious that she was feeling anything but carefree.

It didn't take long for me to figure out why.

"Wait, you still think they're not trying to kill me, don't you? Even after I refused Squirrel Shallix's offer? You still think that, what . . . I'm on their side or something?"

She shook her head too vigorously. "No. I didn't say that."

"You didn't need to say it. I saw it in your eyes."

"Sven, I didn't . . . that's not what I . . ." Her shoulders sagged and she let out a long, slow breath. Then she silently rose to her feet, pulled open the door, and walked out of the bathroom, leaving me alone with everything she didn't say.

I touched the healed area on my shoulder. Other than the ragged hole in my shirt, you'd never have known anything had happened.

I should have been relieved that I healed so quickly.

I wasn't.

The sight of my body doing something so . . . inhuman reminded me of what I was. And what I wasn't. I wasn't a kid. Not really. I was a *thing*. An *it*. Just like the fake Will that got its head blown up in the school yard. I looked just like that on the inside. I didn't have a brain. I had a CPU. I didn't even have a heart. I had a recirculator.

When I raised my head, I was startled by the image of the boy I saw in the mirror. It was me, of course. I didn't look any different than I had just a few days before. But now I somehow felt that it was a stranger staring back at me. A stranger who was just hours away from doing something horrible that would kill every human on Earth. And I had no idea what!

The disconnect between the person I always thought I was and the *thing* I actually was made me feel like I was being torn in two. Alicia and Dr. Shallix might be at war with each other. But me? I was at war with myself.

I blinked back the tears that began pooling in the corners of my eyes and turned my mind to practicalities. Those were easier to think about. Like when the next attack would come. Because it seemed to me that it really was just a question of *when*, not if. I mean, those chickens didn't arrange themselves on plates with a garnish of parsley and lemon wedges, hide themselves under lids, and deliver themselves to our room. Somebody put them there. Somebody who was *in the hotel*.

I bent over to lick the toilet seat nervously, then came out of the bathroom to find Alicia and Will already discussing it.

"Why roast chickens?" Will asked. "Why not just a couple of guys with guns?"

"Think about it," Alicia replied. "It was a sneak attack. They got into our room without creating a commotion. If they had sent a guy to kill us, there's no way we would have just let him in without making a scene. And we know a scene is the last thing Shallix wants. As for guns, they never use them. It's like they think it's wrong to take advantage of lesser machines or something. Or maybe they just like getting up close and personal when they kill people. I don't know. But they always fight hand-to-hand. Or chicken-wing-to-hand, as the case may be."

Alicia stopped talking abruptly and eyed me, unable to let it go.

I sat down on the bed across from her. "You don't really think I'm on their side, do you?" I breathed.

"I didn't say that."

"It's not what you said. It's how you look at me. You don't trust me."

She dropped her gaze to the blue-and-gray-patterned carpet on the floor.

Dead silence filled the room.

I guess I had assumed that by now, Alicia accepted me as an ally. But the look on her face was a blunt reminder that if it came down to it, she'd do what she had to do to save humanity. She'd kill me before she'd let Dr. Shallix get me back. And, of course, Dr. Shallix would probably do something far worse than killing me.

My stomach churned. Alicia wouldn't look me in the eye. It was clear my chances of making it to my thirteenth birthday alive were dropping by the minute.

I wanted to reassure her, convince her that I was on her side. But I couldn't find the words.

My best friend found them for me.

"Come on, Alicia," Will said gently. "This is Sven. He's been like a brother to me for as long as I can remember. He's not trying to hurt anyone. I promise you that. I promise."

He paused to take a deep breath, then continued, his voice beginning to shake. "You know what? When everyone else used to laugh at me and call me names because of my OCD, he always came to my defense. *Always*. In third grade, he got a bottle of glue dumped over his head for telling Brandon Marks to stop calling me Bizarro Boy and Sir Touch-a-Lot. In fourth grade, he got sent to the principal's office for saying *he* was the one who kept hiding all the blue markers in art class so I wouldn't get in trouble, because I used to have this thing against the color blue and kept dropping all the blue markers down the air vent at the back of the room. He was always there for me. I mean, this is Sven we're talking about. He's my best . . ."

Will's bottom lip quivered, and he rubbed his eyes with the back of one huge hand.

Alicia just looked at me without saying a word. Which was good, because the lump in my throat was way too big for me to talk around.

"Listen . . . ," Alicia began after a long silence.

Whatever she was going to say, she didn't get to finish. There was another knock at the door.

CHAPTER 31.0:
\ < value= [I Decide to Get a New Hobby] \ >

"ROOM SERVICE," A MUFFLED VOICE CALLED from the corridor.

We all looked at one another.

Will scrambled to his feet and dashed into the bathroom. The lock clicked loudly. "Uh, you know, I gotta go," he called through the door, his voice quavering.

Alicia stepped over the dead cyborg chickens on the floor and looked through the peephole before cautiously opening the door. A short, balding man with a neat gray mustache waited in the corridor behind a cart loaded with three covered plates.

"Three pepperoni . . ." He trailed off as he noticed the dead birds on the floor.

"Oh, uh, these were a little undercooked," I offered.

Alicia grabbed the cart of food. "Thanks."

She wheeled it inside and slammed the door in in the man's face.

We stared at the three covered plates for probably five minutes. Finally, I lifted one of the covers off. And there on the plate lay a fresh, warm pepperoni pizza.

Over the course of the next half hour, Will lifted every single slice of pepperoni to make sure no earwigs lurked underneath. Alicia watched him with interest.

"What's the deal with that, anyway?" she asked him. "You know, with the stuff and junk."

"What, pepperoni?" Will replied. "You don't have it where you're from? Well, it's really good and it's made out of . . . well, I don't really know what and I don't think I actually want to know."

Alicia laughed. "I know what pepperoni is. I'm talking about your OCD. You know, looking *under* the pepperoni and turning light switches on and off and touching things."

"Ah, right, that." Will tilted his head thoughtfully, drumming his fingers in the usual pattern. Finally, he spoke. "I just have to."

Alicia's eyes widened incredulously. "That's it? You just have to?"

He shrugged. "Yeah, it's hard to explain. But it's just something I have to do. I don't really think about it much. My brain's just wired that way, I guess. Like when I go to bed at night, I always have to go downstairs and make sure the door is locked. Then I sometimes have to go down again and make sure I didn't forget to make sure the door is locked. Oh, and before I get into bed, I have to check my closet."

"Why?" Alicia asked.

"To make sure there are no dead bodies in it," Will said, like it was the most obvious reason in the world.

She scratched her head. "So, do you really think you'll find a dead body in there?"

Will pondered this for a moment. "Only if I don't check. Sven knows what I'm talking about, right?"

"You mean because he eats stuff?" Alicia asked, turning her gaze to me. "You know, Sven, I've been thinking about that ever since I saw you eat that wallpaper. And I don't know if it's actually a glitch in your programming."

I blushed. I hated talking about my unusual eating habits. "What are you talking about? I'm supposed to pass for human, right? Why would I be programmed to do something so unusual if I was supposed to be like everybody else? It doesn't exactly make me fit in. It's got to be a glitch."

"I don't know." She rubbed her temples with her fingers. "That's what I'm trying to figure out. I mean, maybe you're right. Maybe it is just a bug in your code. But it seems too big a thing for the Ticks to miss. They're not perfect, but they're methodical. And they want to keep their secret. If Shallix thought your eating things might clue people in to your being Synthetic, he probably would have . . . gotten rid of you. Unless there's a reason they want you do it. So I think we should be open to the possibility it's deliberate. But the question is why they'd program you that way."

Nobody had an answer.

Talking about myself like I was nothing more than some kind of computer program depressed me. Everything I knew about myself, about who I was, *what* I was . . . it was all wrong. I'd always felt like a normal kid. Okay, maybe like an *abnormal* kid, but a kid all the same. Not some kind of cyborg.

In what felt like a forced casual tone, Alicia suddenly said, "Anyway, you're probably wiped. Why don't you get some sleep, Sven? You, too, Will."

"Do you guys think it's okay to stay here?" I asked. "I mean, what if something . . . tries to kill us again?"

Will's face turned a little gray. He got up to check that the door was locked. Then he sat back down on the bed. Then he got up again and checked the door once more. Finally, before getting back on the bed, he opened the closet door, looked inside for dead bodies, and closed it again.

Alicia tilted her head toward the window. "I'd rather be in here than out there in the dark. And at least there's only one door, so they can't sneak up on us. We can sleep in shifts. One stays awake while the other two sleep. We only have two beds, anyway. I'll take the first shift."

She pulled the chair away from the desk and sat, straight-backed and tense, fingering the razor-sharp edge of her knife.

I couldn't help noticing the grim set of her mouth. And the fact that her gaze kept settling on me, then abruptly darting away as soon as she realized I saw her.

It wasn't easy to sleep knowing that a girl with a big knife was trying not to be seen watching you. Then again, it wasn't easy to sleep knowing that at any moment some other Tick assassins could burst through the door. And if that weren't enough, Will was snoring like a chain saw.

So the fact I fell asleep at all was pretty amazing. But when exhaustion finally forced me into unconsciousness, I found myself in the most vivid dream of my life.

I was back home with my dad, standing in the backyard early on a sunny morning.

"Hey, champ," Dad said, "I've been thinking, football really isn't your game. You know where your talent lies? Sneezing."

"It does?" I asked.

"Jumpin' Jack Nicklaus on a pogo stick, it sure does! Now go ahead and let 'er rip. Give me a big, juicy sneeze."

"Wait, Dad?" I said. "You just want me to sneeze? Why?"

A too-wide smile stretched across my father's face. "Sneezing is a *great* hobby, son! Did you know the world record for the longest sneezing fit is more than two years? I bet you could beat that, Sven! Give it a try!"

"But I can't just sneeze. I've never sneezed in my life. I can't just turn it on like a switch."

A look of anger flashed in Dad's eyes. "You are going to learn to sneeze! It is why you are here, yes?"

"Well, okay, I guess," I said doubtfully. "But it seems kind of like a weird hobby to me."

"It is not weird, Sven," Dad insisted. "All the cool kids are sneezing these days, yes? Now sneeze!"

"Really?"

"Just do it!" Dad yelled.

"But, Dad, I can't sneeze," I told him.

"FOR CRYING OUT LOUD, WILL YOU JUST

SNEEZE ALREADY?" my father screamed.

Suddenly, the air was filled with black pepper. It blew into my eyes and my mouth. I choked and gagged on the fine, dry powder.

"SNEEZE!" my father shrieked. "SNEEZE!"

A sensation I had never experienced before began building in my head. It started in my nose and radiated outward. A ticklish, uncontrollable feeling.

Then I realized what it was. And no matter how hard I fought, I couldn't resist it. I had to . . . .

The impact of the floor at my back knocked the air from my lungs and I forced my eyes open only to see Alicia glaring down at me. The blade of her knife was cold against my throat.

CHAPTER 32.0:
\ < value= [The Sneeze to End All Sneezes] \ >

ON THE TV BEHIND HER, A NEWSCASTER was talking about a fire in an abandoned house on the outskirts of town and the singed rainbow wig firefighters found at the scene.

Will snored peacefully in one of the king-size beds.

"Explain yourself, Tick!" Alicia spat.

"What...what happened?" I stammered, trying to shake my brain out of its slumber. "What are you doing, Alicia?"

"You were talking in your sleep," she snarled. "You were talking about sneezing."

I felt her knife press harder against the flesh of my throat.

"Wait! Hold on! What are you talking about? So what if I was talking in my sleep? I was just having a weird dream, that's all. My dad told me he wanted me to sneeze," I told her. "But why is that so bad? People talk in their sleep all the time!"

She shook her head. "Not like this, they don't. You had his voice."

"Whose voice? What do you mean?"

"You sounded like *him*, Sven. Shallix!"

"But I thought we blocked his signal or something," I protested. "That's why I'm wearing aluminum underwear! You said we blocked the signal!"

"Shut up! Why were you talking like him? Tell me! Has he taken control of you? Why does he want you to sneeze?" She held the knife right up to my face. "Tell me or I'll finish you right now!"

"I don't know! I don't know!" Hot tears began spilling from the corners of my eyes. Anxiety ate away at my self-control, and I felt a terrible compulsion building. I darted my tongue out and licked the flat side of her knife.

She wrinkled her nose. "Eww. Don't lick that! This

knife has been in chickens and clowns, and I used it a couple of days ago to clean dog poop off my sneaker. It's gotta be totally covered in germs. . . ."

Her eyes widened. She stared at me for a few moments, then leapt off me, backing away until she was pressed up against the wall. She held her knife out toward me menacingly.

"Stay away from me!" she hissed.

I sat up. "Alicia, what? I don't under—"

"Shut up! I need to think!"

She began pacing back and forth along the length of the room, muttering to herself in Russian. After traversing the room at least fifty times, she stopped and fingered the blade of her knife, shaking her head slowly.

"*Eto ono*," she muttered. "What else could it be?"

"What's going on? What are you talking about?" I asked, trying to read the complex eddy of emotions on her face.

Alicia took a long, deep, quivery breath and strode over to me. She didn't say a word—just looked at me with a mixture of fear and sadness and revulsion in her eyes.

Her mouth tensed into a thin, straight line. "I'm so sorry, Sven. I don't want to do this."

She knelt and tightened her grip on the knife, holding it, trembling, above the center of my chest.

"I'm so sorry," she said in a hoarse croak. "But I have to. Please understand."

"Wait!" I cried. "Stop! Why are you doing this? Alicia, please don't do this!"

She rubbed her eyes with her free hand. "I don't have a choice. I'm . . . I'm so sorry."

"Why? Is it because I talked in my sleep? I was just dreaming! Honestly, I didn't know I was doing it. Please!"

"It's not that," she said swallowing hard. "*Srok rasplaty*. I just figured out what you're going to do on the day of reckoning. How you're supposed to destroy the human race."

"I don't understand," I whispered.

The news anchor smiled ingratiatingly, his skin tone a little green and pixilated on the TV screen. ". . . Well, Dianne, it looks like that little dog has shown us that you *can* teach an old person new tricks."

She looked at me with wet eyes. "Eating gross things isn't a glitch, Sven. It's what you've been programmed to do. It's what makes you their secret weapon. And the dream, the sneeze . . . it all makes sense now."

"I don't get it," I said. "How does any of that even matter? It was just a dream."

Alicia shook her head. "It matters. Man, I've been so stupid. I should have realized that one kid couldn't kill every human on the planet unless he was . . ."

"He was *what*?" I asked. "What am I?"

"You're a bioweapon, Sven. An incubator," she told me. "That's why you eat gross stuff. You're sampling pathogens."

"What are you talking about?"

She lowered the knife. "Your whole life you've been eating and licking really disgusting things, right? You weren't doing it for fun. It was to get samples of all kinds of nasty stuff. Viruses and bacteria. Your body is programmed to synthesize everything you sample into a supervirus. One that could wipe out the whole human race."

"Hold on," I interjected. "How do you know this?"

"I heard my parents talking about it over dinner one night. Back in the Settlement, years before I was born, the Ticks tried something just like this. It didn't work. The Settlement was small enough that when a new person showed up and started coughing in everyone's face, they immediately realized it was a Tick. They deactivated it before anyone got sick. With you, I guess they had a better strategy. They created you as a baby, here in Schenectady. You went to school, acted like a normal human. Nobody would have any idea you were cooking up something that could kill them all."

"But I don't understand," I said. "If I'm supposed to be carrying this superkiller virus, how come no one around me has gotten sick yet? Heck, *I've* never even been sick. I've never even sneezed before. Ever."

"I don't know. I guess it takes a long time to sample enough stuff to create a disease that's really deadly or something," she told me.

"Like thirteen years. My thirteenth birthday. Just like Dr. Shallix said."

"And that sneeze you were dreaming about, Sven? That's your mission. That's why you dreamed your father told you to sneeze. You're getting ready to deploy the supervirus. That sneeze is what's going to wipe out the human race."

CHAPTER 33.0:

\ < value= [I'm Saved by a Giant Toilet] \ >

MY HEAD STARTED TO SPIN. I DIDN'T want to believe what Alicia was telling me. But as much as I wanted to deny it, a nagging little voice in my head told me it was all true. I was the ultimate biological weapon. The whole reason I was alive was to destroy humanity.

The news anchor's voice broke through my shock. "...after being stuck in the car wash for nine hours, the man was finally rescued by firefighters."

Alicia slowly raised her knife, wrapping both hands tightly around the handle. "Now you know why I have to do this, Sven. You have something inside you that can kill *everybody*. And it's going to be unleashed on your birthday, which at this point is less than twenty-four hours away. Please understand. I know you're a good kid. I wish this didn't have to happen. I wish . . . I wish we could just be friends."

"Wait," I sobbed. "Can't I just go away? Where there's no one around for me to get sick? Like, live in a desert or the North Pole or something? Please?"

She shook her head. "You wouldn't stay there. If Shallix managed to hack into your CPU, he'd be able to control you, Sven. Just like he tried to do tonight. Every time you went to sleep, you'd be at risk. I have to do this."

A tear ran down her cheek. Her jaw was rigid with tension, and I could tell she was fighting to stop her hands from shaking.

She's really going to do this, I thought in disbelief. *This is it. I'm going to die.*

The news anchor continued to prattle, his voice carefree yet emotionless. A stark contrast to the terror roiling inside my chest.

". . . He calls his creation Flushosaurus Rex. His Niagara Falls, New York, neighbors may not be thrilled that the former Ukrainian research scientist Sambor Ivanovitch Kozakov, or Junkman Sam, as he calls himself, has built a twenty-foot-tall replica of a toilet in their town. But Sam himself says it's all about artistic expression."

The scientist's heavily accented voice came through the TV speaker. "Those who question my art simply don't understand it. My creation may look like a toilet, but it makes a serious statement about consumption and waste in today's world."

"Fair enough," the reporter continued. "But what people in the town object to is that Sam filled his replica toilet with *actual* human waste. Twenty-two thousand gallons of it, to be precise."

I tried to shut out the sound coming from the TV. I didn't want the last thing I heard to be a story about a giant toilet.

I thought about my mom and dad. How much I'd miss them. I braced myself, closing my eyes tightly against my gathering tears, which squeezed out between my eyelids and ran down the sides of my face, collecting in the hollows of my ears before dripping onto the carpet.

After several seconds, I realized I wasn't dead. I opened my eyes a tiny bit and saw, through a blurry film of tears, the knife still poised above my chest. It trembled in Alicia's hands. I looked at her face. She was staring into space, lost in deep concentration.

What was she waiting for? *Just get it over with!*

She looked down at me, then, without warning, threw the knife down. She grabbed the sides of my face tightly, pulled me into a sitting position, and leaned in close.

"Sambor Ivanovitch Kozakov!" she cried, with a giddy laugh. "Junkman Sam!"

I stared at her. Maybe I was dead and this was some kind of afterlife in which everyone said things that made no sense.

"Um, what-man-who?"

Her eyes glowed. "Junkman Sam! Listen, Sven. There might be a way to fix this!"

I sat up straight. "You mean *without* killing me?"

She nodded. "There was this scientist. He worked in Laboratoriya 54u. Sambor Ivanovitch Kozakov. He was miles ahead of everyone in the field of artificial intelligence. It was his work that made self-aware machines possible. But he was convinced that what he was doing would eventually get out of control. That machine evolution would outpace ours and put the entire human race at risk. One day he just kinda went crazy. Disappeared. Took off and went into hiding. By then it was too late and . . . well, you know what happens next."

I scratched my head. "So what does that have to do with a giant toilet?"

"Nobody knew for sure what happened to the guy. But there was this rumor that when he lost his marbles, he moved to America and changed his name and started building all kinds of crazy stuff that he called 'art.'"

"So, wait," I said. "He's . . ."

"Junkman Sam," she said. "The guy on the news story. He basically invented the neural network that all Ticks have. If we can find him, he might be able to change your programming or take out your virus processing unit or whatever the heck you have."

"Wait!" I snorted. "You're telling me my life depends

on a guy named *Junkman Sam*? Great! While we're at it, why don't we stop to see Hobo Bill to pick up a cure for cancer? Oh, I'm sure Poop Chute Larry could hook us up with a way to—"

I never saw the slap coming. Alicia's open hand connected with my face hard enough to stop my words cold.

My left cheek burned and stung as if it had been attacked by a swarm of angry bees. "Ow! What? What'd I do?"

"You just don't get it, do you?" she hissed, her eyes gleaming with tears. "You just don't get it! I finally discover a reason why I may not have to kill you, and you treat it like some kind of joke?"

She slumped down and swiped the back of her hand across her eyes. It came away wet.

"I don't want to kill you, Sven. Don't you understand that? Just the thought of it . . ." A sob overwhelmed her.

A cold jolt rippled through my chest. What a jerk I was. I always assumed my fate meant nothing to Alicia. I was just another Tick. The enemy. A machine. Yet even though she'd had plenty of opportunities to kill me, here

I was, in a fancy hotel, alive and still perfectly capable of sticking my foot in my mouth. And it was all because of her.

"Alicia, I'm sorry," I whispered. "I just thought . . . well, I guess I didn't think. I'm sorry. I didn't mean to be a jerk."

I didn't see the next slap coming either.

"Hey! What was that for? I said I was sorry," I cried, rubbing my right cheek.

"That was advance payment for next time," she responded, back to her usual unflappable self. Her eyes shone bright and cold and tearless. "Now, are you ready to find Junkman Sam? Or should we just skip right to the end of the world?"

I swallowed and then smiled weakly. "I've always liked meeting new people."

"We're meeting new people?" Will said groggily, from his bed. He sat up and rubbed the gunk out of his eyes. "What's going on?" he said. "I was having the best dream about soap."

"Road trip," Alicia told him. "Let's go."

CHAPTER 34.0:
\ < value= [We Take the Barf Bus to Vomit Town] \ >

"WHERE ARE WE GOING?" WILL ASKED AS we walked toward the bus station, the rosy light of the rising sun making his hair look even redder than usual—like a tangle of highly embarrassed earthworms had taken up residence on his head.

"Niagara Falls," Alicia replied matter-of-factly.

Will lifted his eyebrows and looked sideways at her. "Okay, why?"

"To see a twenty-foot-high toilet," I told him, as if it were the most natural thing in the world to do when a bunch of deadly cyborgs were out to kill you and everybody else on the planet.

We walked the rest of the way to the bus station in silence.

Which gave me plenty of time to think about things I didn't really want to think about. Like the fact that the rest of my life might be measured not in years, but in hours. That we had until midnight to find a way to stop me from killing the entire population of Earth. And that the only beings I had anything in common with were roast chickens and clown snakes and a psycho pediatrician.

Even if we managed to foil my mission to destroy humanity, that sobering fact wasn't going to change. I would always be different from everyone else I knew. I'd be something else. Not really human. Not entirely machine.

Even with my best friend walking right next to me, I'd never felt so lonely in my whole life.

I looked up to find Alicia watching me, a look of concern as plain as day on her face. But her pity only made me feel worse.

I scowled back at her, and in an instant, her concern morphed into that standard Alicia Toth brand of guarded indifference.

We arrived at the bus station, a stark hardscape of cement floors and fluorescent-lit benches. "I hate to tell you this," Will said, "but a bus to Niagara Falls is going to cost more than twelve dollars and fifty-eight cents."

"Oh, yeah?" Alicia pointed to a kiosk at the end of the station. A big sign on the top of it read:

>>>—BULLET BUS—>

A SUBSIDIARY OF CHEEP-O-RIDE, INC.
ASK ABOUT OUR $1 FARES

We made our way through the station and approached the kiosk. The Bullet Bus ticket agent was busy talking on his cell phone and completely ignored us. Alicia cleared her throat loudly. The agent gave her a dirty look, hung up his phone, and peered at us from behind a filthy, scratched-up Plexiglas ticket window.

"Yeah?" he said listlessly, barely bothering to lift his head.

"We'd like three one-dollar tickets to Niagara Falls, please," Alicia said confidently.

The agent studied her under half-closed eyelids. "Yeah, we got some one-dollar tickets left. You gotta help out on the bus to get them, though."

"Help out?" I asked. "You mean like work? What would we have to do?"

"Whatever the driver asks you to do. Hand out snacks and junk, I guess," he replied in a monotone.

Alicia dug three one-dollar bills out of her backpack. "That's fine. Three to Niagara Falls, please."

"Hold on," the man said. "You gotta be eighteen to ride without a parent. Are you guys eighteen?"

We all nodded.

"Oh, yeah? If you're eighteen, when were you born?"

"Uh," Alicia muttered, "um, we were born eighteen years ago."

I elbowed her.

The agent eyed her suspiciously. We could practically see the little hamster wheel turning in his head as he mulled Alicia's answer over. Finally, he shrugged and handed us three tickets.

"Bus don't leave 'til noon. Better make yourselves comfy."

I looked around the station. The ancient bare wood benches that lined the walls looked about as welcoming as a row of guillotines. Make ourselves comfy? Yeah, right.

We spent the next several hours eating stale food out of the station's sole vending machine and taking turns complaining about how much the cruel, unupholstered benches made our butts hurt.

When it was finally time to board the bus, we immediately wished we had decided to walk the three hundred miles to Niagara Falls. Our shoes clung to the sticky floors, and every seat was adorned with a patchwork of peeling silver duct tape. But worst of all? The smell. My nostrils burned with the reek of stale vomit. Of course, that didn't stop me from ripping off a scrap of torn vinyl from one of the seats and popping it in my mouth. *Yech!*

A massively obese man didn't so much sit in the driver's seat as ooze over the edges of it. He took our tickets and looked us up and down. "Oh, goody. My flight attendants are here." He laughed wheezily at his own joke, then thrust a stack of empty brown paper bags at us. "Hand these out to all the passengers."

"What are they for?" I asked.

"You'll know when you know," the driver grunted.

We slowly walked the length of the bus, handing out bags to each of our fellow passengers. Most of them turned to us only briefly, before resuming staring numbly at the backs of the seats in front of them. When we were sure each rider had a bag, we took the only remaining seats all the way at the back of the bus.

We soon found out what the bags were for. The driver started the engine and pulled the bus onto the street. Thanks to a bad shock absorber, it bucked this way and that, like a boat being tossed on a rough sea.

The minute we hit the New York State Thruway, a little old lady in the third row began to barf. Her guttural retching set off a chain reaction among the passengers behind her, until row after row of travelers were heaving into their paper bags.

"What are you flight attendants waiting for?" the driver bellowed. "Pick up the full ones and hand out more empty ones!"

We spent the entire seven-hour trip lugging bags of puke up and down the aisle, storing them in overhead compartments, under seats, wherever we could find space.

Well, that's actually not entirely true. We didn't spend the *whole* trip carrying bags of barf. We spent quite a bit of time filling our own bags as well.

CHAPTER 35.0:
\ < value= [We Hang Out at the Mall] \ >

WE TOTTERED OFF THE BUS EARLY THAT
evening in front of an old auto body shop. Niagara Falls
wasn't anything like I had imagined it. The street was
webbed with cracks and lined with boarded-up shops
that were practically crumbling from age and neglect.
Somewhere in the distance, a dog barked.

We took a moment to get our bearings.

I scratched my head. "Where do you think we'll find
Junkman Sam? Should we just go door to door looking
for a twenty-foot-tall toilet?"

"Check this out, guys," Will said. He pointed to something on a map of the town attached to the bus stop sign.

It was faded from the weather and a little tough to read behind its cloudy plastic holder, but if you leaned in and squinted, you could just make out the words WORLD'S LARGEST next to a little blue star on the map. It said something after WORLD'S LARGEST, but no matter how hard we looked, we couldn't make it out.

"That has to be Flushosaurus Rex," Alicia said confidently. "I mean, how many world's largest things could there be in this town?"

"I don't know," I replied. "It's Niagara Falls. How about world's largest waterfall?"

"Actually, Niagara Falls isn't even in the top ten largest," Will pointed out. "It's number eleven in terms of volume."

When he noticed us looking at him, he added, "What? I have a thing about waterfalls. It's kind of a hobby."

Alicia stared at me until I said it: "Fine, it's probably the toilet. Let's go."

Alicia took another look at the map and slid her phone out of her backpack. Once she had tapped the location into a GPS app, we set off in the direction of the blue star. We followed the little GPS voice—its cheerful tone oblivious to the fact that doomsday was just a few hours away—as it directed us down various streets, across a baseball field covered with knee-high weeds, and past a closed bowling alley.

Eventually, it announced that we were nearing our destination.

We emerged from an overgrown wooded path at the edge of an abandoned shopping mall parking lot. The wide stretch of asphalt looked like the splintered shell of a hard-boiled egg, with big slabs of pavement jutting up here and there. A whole fleet of rusty, forgotten shopping carts were strewn about at random. A sign that read NIAGARA CENTER MALL hung at an angle off a pair of girders that jutted out from the ground. I half expected zombies to come shuffling out of the deteriorating building moaning, *BRRRAAAIIINNNNS*.

"So, where's the potty?" I asked. "I kinda figured it would be hard to miss."

It turns out the little blue star hadn't marked the

location of the world's biggest toilet. Instead, Alicia's GPS had brought us to something else entirely.

We looked around but couldn't find a single giant toilet. We did find a sign next to the mall entrance, though. It read:

NIAGARA CENTER MALL
Home of the World's Largest Ball of Dental Floss

Started in 1963 by Niagara Falls native and floss-o-maniac Franklin Goddard Watts, this national treasure is now nearly six feet in diameter and weighs just over six thousand pounds.

Please do not touch the ball of floss.

No smoking near the ball of floss.

Do not unravel the ball of floss.

Pets are not permitted on or near the ball of floss.

We hope you love our ball of floss as much as we do!

"Okay, so not a toilet," Alicia sighed. "What now?"

"Can we go check out the floss?" Will asked.

"Dude," I said, "it's a ball of string."

"No," he corrected. "It's the world's largest ball of *floss*. When will we have the chance to see it again?"

"If it were up to me, never," Alicia grumbled. "Besides, we're not here to sightsee. We only have a few hours to find Junkman Sam."

Will got a sort of sad-puppy-dog look in his eyes. "Just five minutes. . . ."

I looked at Alicia. She shrugged. "I guess we could use a few minutes to regroup and figure out where to look next."

"Fine," I sighed. "Let's go see the string."

Alicia crouched down next to the gate that guarded the mall doors and forced it open with her crowbar. Its rusted metal gave way easily.

We stepped inside, shards from a shattered glass door crunching beneath our feet.

Inside, it was dark. Alicia snapped on a flashlight. And then . . .

My heart almost stopped.

We were surrounded by zombies!

CHAPTER 36.0:

\ < value= [We Manage to Keep Our Brains] \ >

IN SPITE OF ALL THE HORRIBLE THINGS we had faced over the last few days, I didn't think I'd ever heard Alicia scream in pure terror.

That was exactly what she did when she saw the pale, bald, inhuman faces staring at us in the faint glow of the flashlight.

She freaked, leaping across the mall's deserted vestibule to attack a row of the ghastly, waxen creatures with her crowbar, shrieking wildly, spinning, slashing, kicking. She swung the steel tool at a particularly scary-looking figure in a cheap-looking tuxedo, and the creature's head exploded. Shards of plastic rained down upon us.

Because what Alicia was trying to beat the life out of wasn't a zombie at all—it was a mannequin.

We had stumbled into the men's clothing section of an old department store.

There were no zombies. Only a legion of harmless plastic people. Sure, in the gloomy, abandoned mall, blanketed with a thick layer of dust and cobwebs, they were creepy as heck. But they probably wouldn't be eating anyone's brains.

"Stop!" I yelled over the crunch of plastic limbs.

"Aaaaahhhhh!" she screamed, her voice dripping with fear and rage. "Zombies! Run!"

I picked a severed mannequin head up off the floor and held it out for her to see. "Look, no zombies. Calm down."

Her crowbar was a silver blur in the dim light. *Whack!* It connected with the head, batting it out of my hand and across the room. It hit the concrete floor, ricocheted off an old sales counter, and came to rest at Will's feet. He looked down, let out a feeble squeak, and collapsed to the ground in a faint.

I stepped in front of Alicia, my arms raised. "It's okay! Stop!"

There was no light of recognition in her eyes— only a kind of animal fear. She was operating purely on instinct, incapable of distinguishing me from a plastic clothes model. She raised the crowbar over her head and brought it down with a scream of fury. I dove to the right. Sparks leapt off the concrete where the tool struck with a loud metallic *clank*. She brought the bar back up and stood over me, panting, staring at me with wild, panicked eyes.

"Alicia," I pleaded. "It's me, Sven. Put down the crowbar. Please."

A strangled sob escaped her lips, and she let the crowbar clank to the floor. Slumping down on a bench against the wall, she exhaled, a long, shaky breath that seemed to take with it her energy. She tilted her head back against the wall and stared up at the water-stained ceiling tiles.

Years ago, bored kids probably sat right where Alicia was now. Maybe they counted those very ceiling tiles as they waited impatiently for their parents to finish trying on clothes.

The thought of my mom, who had dragged me along on countless boring errands as well, sitting hundreds of miles away at a dinner table with a lousy Tick replica of me, practically knocked my feet out from under me.

I sat down heavily next to Alicia. "I wish I was home."

"I wish I *had* a home," she said, burying her face in her hands.

Suddenly, the room didn't feel creepy anymore. Just depressing.

I put my hand on her shoulder. This time she didn't smack it away. I could feel her body shake with silent, convulsive sobs.

"My whole life," she choked out between labored gasps, "I've been taught that Ticks are less than human. That they're the enemy. That every single one of them would kill me just as soon as look at me. You're not supposed to get attached to them. You're not supposed to care about them. And here you are, the one Synthetic that can wipe out every human on the planet . . . and you happen to be the closest thing I even have to a friend." She laughed humorlessly. "How pathetic am I? It's like my life has become some cheesy made-for-TV movie."

"We're friends?" I muttered aloud, taken aback hearing that term uttered by the girl who had recently compared me to a toaster. "I . . . I . . ." I searched my head for words to offer her. None of them were right. "Alicia, I don't know what to say. I'm . . . I'm sorry."

"I'm the one who should be sorry. I said some pretty awful things about you before. I shouldn't have done that. You're not just a machine. I feel like garbage for the way I treated you." She sighed heavily. "I don't even deserve to have a friend like you. I'm such a *tupitsa*."

I raised my eyebrows. "*Tupi*-what?"

"*Tupitsa*. It means loser. Outcast. Bonehead. That's what everyone back home thought about me. The whole school. Probably even my parents—even though they never said it."

I didn't understand why she was suddenly so down on herself. She seemed like the coolest, most confident kid I'd ever met. I told her that.

"Yeah, that was the one good thing about coming to this country," she replied. "Nobody knew me. I could reinvent myself. But back home, everyone hated me. That's why I always kept to myself. I figured I could keep people from finding out what a *tupitsa* I was. Didn't matter. I tried to act all superbad, and here I am, scared of a bunch of plastic mannequins. I'm still just a big loser."

"Why would everyone hate you?" I asked. "I don't hate you, and you've been trying to kill me."

I meant it as a joke, but she didn't crack a smile.

"Back home there was . . . an incident a couple of years before I came here," she told me, staring at the floor. "It was my fault. In the Settlement I'm from, there were no pets allowed. No animals of any kind. They were strict about it too. Any animals they found, they'd put outside the walls—or worse. I always thought it was a stupid rule. Anyway, I was outside the walls with my friends one day and I found this tiny baby bunny. It was hurt, bleeding. My friends told me to forget about it, that I'd get in trouble. I tried to forget. But I couldn't get that little bunny out of my head. So that night, I snuck out and brought it inside."

"Wait," I interrupted. "Everyone hated you because of a baby rabbit?"

She looked at me sadly. "I wanted to nurse it back to health and let it go again. I wasn't going to keep it or anything. I put it in a cardboard box under my bed and then went to sleep. When I woke up in the morning, it was gone. At first I thought my parents found it and turned it in. But then I heard the news."

She grabbed her braids and pulled on them. Her eyes glinted with anguish. "It was a Tick," she spat. "By the time they deactivated it, it had killed six people. *Six!* All because of me."

"But how could you have known? It was just a bunny."

"I should have known. But like you said, thinking was never my strong suit. I was so stupid. When people found out what I did, no one would talk to me. The kids at school totally shunned me."

"I know what that's like," I told her.

"After that, all I wanted to do was get back at those lousy Ticks for what they had done to me. I started taking extra combat instruction. I learned how to fight."

"You are pretty great at fighting," I mumbled in a feeble attempt to make her feel better.

She snorted disdainfully and looked down at the smashed plastic figures on the floor. "After a couple of years, I thought I was *so* tough. That's when I stole a Tick popper and snuck off to try to find some Ticks."

She paused and closed her eyes tightly, like she was trying to shut out some awful memory.

"The problem is, I did. They weren't far from the Settlement. I should have just run back and told someone. But I seem to have this talent for doing the wrong thing. I tried to take them out myself. I took careful aim with the popper. I figured I'd get the biggest one first. I slowly squeezed the trigger. And missed by a mile. All I managed to do was make them angry.

"They started to move toward me. I was so scared, I just dropped the Tick popper and ran like crazy. When I stopped, I realized I was lost. It took me hours to get back to the Settlement. And when I did, it was . . . gone. They'd killed everyone. Burned most of the buildings. And it was all my fault."

"You can't blame yourself," I whispered. "You—"

"*Of course I can blame myself!*" she snapped. "All I've ever done is screw things up. And now I think I can just show up here and save the world. That if I act all tough and confident, people won't realize what a loser I am. That I can hide who I really am behind some make-believe tough-girl armor. Yeah, right. What a *tupitsa*. I don't know what I was thinking."

I didn't know what say, so we sat in silence until I cleared my throat awkwardly. "We should probably get going. We don't have much time."

She let out a slow, shuddering sigh. "What's the point? I'm scared of mannequins. I'm scared of Ticks. I'm scared of what will happen if I screw up again. It won't just be the Settlement this time. It'll be the whole world. I'm just not good enough to do this. I'm . . . done."

She covered her face with her hands and let out a long, despondent moan.

Seeing her like this set off an ache deep within my chest. I'd always thought she was so perfectly cool, so tough. Like some kind of invincible machine—the definition of awesome. But all of a sudden she seemed . . . more human. More vulnerable. And the thing is, it made her even more awesome. Knowing that she might have been frightened on the inside but could still be so brave and capable on the outside. It wasn't her combat training that made her strong. It was that despite the doubts about herself, she had the courage to give everything she had to take on problems that were so much bigger than she was.

I glanced over at the girl sitting next to me—the strongest person I had ever met. The ache in my chest grew into something bigger. Something that flooded my whole body with a hot, restless energy and flushed away the fear.

I got to my feet and kicked a severed mannequin arm across the floor.

"You know what? *You* may not feel like you're good enough. But *I* know you are," I told her, untapped anger suddenly rising to the surface. "I've had to live my entire life feeling like I wasn't good enough! I suck at throwing a football! I'm the biggest joke in Schenectady because of what I eat! I've never once stood up to the bully who has made my life a misery since third grade! But the last couple of days, as horrible as they've been, have taught me something. They've taught me that no matter how much you might want to sit there and worry about what other people think of you and stress about the mistakes you might have made, you're the only you you've got! And you have to accept it! The only way being different makes you a loser is if you let it!"

She looked up at me with tearstained cheeks.

"So listen to me," I continued. "If you're not going to fight, fine. I will. Because I think *you're* worth fighting for. So stay here if you want. I'm going to find Junkman Sam."

Alicia went utterly still for a moment. Then she blinked through her tears, her shoulders straightening as she finally seemed to register what I'd said.

I could imagine how it had been for her, battling alone for so long with no one to believe in her. But I believed. And I willed the power of my belief—in her courage, in her strength, in her awesomeness—to pour right through me until she couldn't help but see it in my eyes.

She sniffed and cocked an incredulous brow at me. And then it happened.

A smile broke out on her face, so wide and full that it seemed to melt away the shadows in the dingy abandoned mall.

I was just adjusting to the weird feeling of free fall that took hold of my chest when, without warning, Alicia jumped up from the bench and threw her arms around me.

I could still hear the smile in her voice as she spoke beside my ear.

"If you think you can do this without me, you're out of your mind." She squeezed me harder. "Now let's go kick some butt."

And at that moment, I felt like I could have taken on anyone—Dr. Shallix, Pumpkin . . . maybe even Brandon Marks.

CHAPTER 37.0:
\ < value= [Trespassers Will Be . . . What?] \ >

"HEY, WHAT ARE YOU TWO DOING?"

Will stared at us, sitting up surrounded by broken mannequins on the floor.

Alicia and I quickly let go of each other.

"Nothing," we blurted in unison.

Good thing the lighting wasn't better. I could feel myself blushing like a boiled lobster.

I looked at Alicia. She stifled a laugh and wiped her cheeks with the sleeves of her shirt. When she looked up, her eyes glinted with purpose. "If you're done with your nap, Will, we need to find Junkman Sam. Let's move."

"But . . . but . . . we never saw the ball of floss!" Will protested.

Alicia ignored him, abruptly slung her backpack over her shoulder, and headed for the exit.

We walked out into the open air, and Will squinted against the setting sun.

"So how are we going to find him?" he asked.

Before anyone could answer, a gentle wind picked up and rustled the leaves of the overgrown trees that ringed the parking lot. I was expecting a nice fresh breeze. But I got a nose full of stench.

"Eww," I gagged. "What is that?"

"You know what it kind of smells like?" Alicia asked thoughtfully.

Will nodded slowly, his fingers pinching his nose. "A twenty-foot-tall toilet?"

It seemed like a safe bet. I licked my finger and held it up. "The wind is coming from that way," I said pointing to the far side of the lot.

We crossed over the shattered blacktop, weaving between rusted shopping carts, and walked into the woods, letting our noses lead us toward the repulsive smell.

We trudged forward in silence, each of us occupied with our own thoughts. My mind swam with a sea of "what-ifs." What if we didn't find Junkman Sam? What if he couldn't help me? What if reprogramming me ended up scrambling my brain? Would I know who I was anymore? Would I know Mom and Dad? Would I even be me anymore?

I peered at the setting sun glinting through the trees. *If this goes wrong*, I thought, a hard knot of fear tightening beneath my ribs, *I might not see it rise again tomorrow.*

The smell grew stronger and stronger. It reminded me of the time I used the bathroom right after my dad on Chili Dog Wednesday at Giuseppe's Dog and Burger Factory. We were getting close.

When the odor was strong enough to bring tears to our eyes, Alicia stopped at the edge of a little dirt road that cut thorough the woods. She pointed to our right, where it curved around and stopped right in front of a ten-foot-tall chain-link fence covered with razor wire. Jutting up into the air behind it was something big. And toilet-shaped.

"Is that . . . ?" I began.

"Flushosaurus Rex," Alicia finished. "We found it."

I, for one, had never been so glad to see a twenty-foot-high toilet in my life. I started to walk toward it. Alicia stopped me.

"Hold up," she said. "Let's watch for a minute."

The place was clearly an old junkyard. Here and there, tall stacks of rusted, junky cars—even taller than Flushosaurus Rex—towered above the ground. Three squat, corrugated metal buildings sat among them. And an ancient-looking crane loomed above the whole scene.

We sat at the margin of the woods, studying the compound, looking for anything that might be suspicious. Nothing moved.

"No signs of life," Alicia announced after five minutes.

I didn't like the sound of that. "Is that good or bad?"

"Depends." She picked up a rock and tossed it half-heartedly at a clump of coarse grass. "On whether the Ticks got here before us."

Will reached for a broken twig and began feverishly snapping off half-inch lengths, whimpering softly as the pieces fell to the ground.

"We should split up. Each check a building for Junkman Sam," Alicia said at last. "It'll be faster that way. I'll take the middle one. Sven, go left. Will, you search the one on the right. You guys ready?"

"Listen," I said to her, "whatever happens, I just wanted to say . . . thanks. You took a chance on me. You didn't have to. I owe you—"

"Nothing," she interrupted. "You don't owe me anything. This is what I'm here for."

I looked her in the eye for a moment. "No. You were here to kill me, remember? Thanks for, you know, not doing that."

She smiled weakly. "The day's not over yet. Don't get ahead of yourself."

Then she did something I didn't expect. She leaned

in close and kissed me on the cheek. Even though the light was fading with the setting sun, I'm pretty sure you could have seen me blushing a mile away.

Will wrapped his gangly arms around the two of us. Then we just stood there for a few seconds, looking like a trio of complete idiots. Luckily, there was no one there to see us.

Even if there had been, though, I wouldn't have cared.

Will let us go and we stalked quietly through the tall grass, each of us folded into a low crouch, trying to blend in with the vegetation until we reached the front gate. A big weatherworn sign loomed above it.

WELCOME TO JUNKMAN SAM'S SECRET COMPOUND.
TRESPASSERS WILL BE S

The last word looked like it had been hit with a blast from a shotgun. We couldn't make it out.

"Maybe it says 'served a nice cold glass of lemonade,'" Will suggested hopefully.

I got the feeling he was wrong about that.

"If you get into trouble, scream," Alicia told us.

"I think I can manage that," Will replied in a shaky voice.

Alicia carefully pushed the gate open and crept through. Will and I slunk after her. Well, I slunk after her. Will was busy compulsively flipping the gate latch up and down. It screeched ominously on its rusty hinge, like the sound you'd hear when someone opened the basement door in a horror movie. Alicia and I stopped and glared back at him.

When he noticed us, he shrugged and said, "It's not a light switch, but it will have to do."

Alicia and I waited impatiently while Will flipped the latch forty-seven times. Then he joined us.

The path to the center of the compound was only about fifty yards long. But it was the longest walk of my life. I was sure that every step was taking me closer to a hidden Tick or heavily armed mad Ukrainian scientist. But by the time we stood in front of the first building, we'd still seen no sign of any living being—human or otherwise.

"Listen, guys," Alicia said. "Be careful, okay?"

I tried to put on a brave smile. But in reality, I was pretty scared. This was the moment of truth. By the end of the day, I'd either walk out of here and live the rest of my life, or . . . .

"Let's go," I managed to say.

Alicia gave a businesslike nod and, without any further ado, struck off in the direction of the middle building.

Will bit his lip nervously and gestured toward the structure on the right. "Well, I guess that's mine."

He took a few tentative steps, but then stopped to look back at me. I had to pretend I wasn't just as freaked-out as he looked, so I gave him a confident thumbs-up. He straightened his shoulders and continued on his way.

As I approached, I studied the building I was supposed to search. It had definitely seen better days. The metal walls were streaked with rust, and the roof was so bent and dented that I imagined it had been pounded by hailstones the size of bowling balls.

I tried the doorknob. It was unlocked. The door squawked like an enraged elephant when I pushed it open. So much for stealth. I stood in the doorway, waiting for something to happen. Surely, anyone who might have been in the building would have heard that door opening.

But I was met with silence.

I squinted into the gloomy interior. It was too dark to make anything out. So I felt around on the wall for a light switch. When I found one, I flipped it up. The room filled with the hum of electricity as rows of huge overhead lights snapped on. I winced against the sudden brightness.

When my eyes adjusted, I could make out the features of the building. It was basically a warehouse. Just one huge room with a whole bunch of metal beams holding the roof up.

Strange, half-finished sculptures occupied nearly every inch of the place. To my left, an eight-foot-high replica of the Statue of Liberty made out of what looked like old circuit boards and aluminum foil jutted up from a collection of tangled wires. To my right, I saw a small car that had six legs, rather than wheels. It reminded me of a huge beetle.

The weirdest thing, though, stood right in the middle of the room. An immense sculpture of a purple mushroom with a big, fat, green caterpillar smiling down at me from the top. At first, I thought it might be an actual living caterpillar. It pulsated and shuddered as it stared at me unblinkingly. But I soon realized it was mechanical. I could hear the *whir* and *click* of gears as it throbbed on its purple perch.

I had no idea why someone would build something like that. Then again, he was called Junkman Sam. "Junk" pretty well described what I saw scattered around the building. I shouldn't have been surprised. I mean, the guy spent years of his life making a giant toilet. But it didn't make me too optimistic about the chances of his being able to reprogram me. Because, you know, it wasn't like I was a big, smiling caterpillar.

It didn't take me long to search the building. It was empty.

I walked back to the door and turned out the lights. As soon as I stepped outside, I heard something. Alicia's voice.

"Sven!" she screamed. "Sven!"

Then the vicious roar of a gunshot split the air.

CHAPTER 38.0:
\ < value= [I Don't Know Art,
but I Know What Stinks] \ >

MY HEART POUNDED AND MY LEGS WERE

a blur of motion as I sprinted toward the sound. It came
from the building Alicia was searching.

I made it to the door and barely slowed down. Seizing the handle, I yanked it open and rushed through.

Inside, the building was almost identical to the one I
had just left. The same large open room, the same bright
lights. The only difference was that, instead of being filled
with sculptures, this one had big half-painted canvases lying
just about everywhere. Some hung on the walls; others stood
on easels. There were a few dozen just scattered on the floor.

The subject matter of the paintings varied. None of them were very good. But they were all sort of scary. Some showed vicious-looking robots attacking cowering humans. Some showed vicious-looking humans attacking robots. And some showed sad-looking clowns. Those were the scariest.

But what really impressed me was the double-barreled shotgun that was aimed at my face.

The man who held it was short and round and had long, wild, gray hair that looked like he had just stuck a fork in an electrical outlet. Dark welding goggles were perched on his forehead, and he more than filled out his shabby, paint-spattered white shirt and threadbare khaki pants.

"Hi, Sven," Alicia said in a perfectly unconcerned voice. "Good news. I found him. This is Junkman Sam."

I stared at the weapon the man was holding. It was close enough to my face that I could smell the spicy, metallic odor of spent gunpowder hanging heavy at the end of the barrel. My tongue darted out and licked the hot steel.

"Are you okay, Alicia?" I asked, unable to take my eyes off the gun. "Did he hurt you?"

"What?" she answered. "Why would you think he hurt me?"

"You screamed, Alicia! And he's holding a gun! And there was a gunshot! What am I supposed to think?"

The man laughed and waved the shotgun. "This? No, no. This is part of my latest series of paintings. Watch."

He aimed the gun at a handful of spray-paint cans positioned in front of a large canvas.

The shotgun erupted, belching flame. The cans of spray paint exploded into a multicolored mist that spattered the canvas.

Junkman Sam laughed as rivulets of paint ran across the floor and pooled near his feet. "Beautiful, isn't it?"

"Yeah. Very nice," I replied. In fairness, it was a heck of a lot nicer than the clowns.

He swept an arm across the expanse of canvases. "Do you like them? Since I left the field of robotics, I've dedicated myself to art. It's my passion."

I stared at a painting of a sad clown crying as he

smashed a cream pie into another sad clown's face. "Uh, I'm really . . . impressed."

Reloading the gun, Sam smiled at us with a mouthful of teeth that looked like they hadn't seen a toothbrush in years.

"So, listen, Mr. Kozakov," Alicia began. "We need to—"

Before she could finish, the door of the building creaked open.

I heard Alicia's blade slide out of its sheath. Her muscles tensed. Her eyes focused intently on the potential target coming through the door.

But it was only Will.

He pushed the door back on its rusty hinges. "Hey, guys? You in here?" he called.

His eyes bulged as he noticed the menacing black firearm in Junkman Sam's hands.

"No!" Will screamed. "Don't hurt them!"

He picked up a small painting of a robot clown chasing a human clown and hurled it at its creator. It shot through the air and, as if it were a pants-guided missile, hit Sam right in the you-know-whats.

The shotgun fell through the air and landed butt down on the concrete floor.

Both barrels thundered as the weapon discharged toward the ceiling.

Jagged shards of glass rained down on us from the huge banks of overhead lights. A terrible, metallic groaning sound echoed around the space. Then the noise of an entire row of heavy industrial light fixtures crashing to the ground nearly shredded my eardrums.

Sparks crackled and flew from the wires that had been connected to the lights, but were now simply lying on the floor. The current flowing through them made them slither around like long black snakes. One of the wires flopped into a large puddle of spilled paint that had collected in the center of the room.

WHOOMP!

My skin stung as heat and light blazed around us.

"Run!" Alicia shouted.

The three of us burst out of the burning building and fell in a heap on the ground.

A second later, Junkman Sam waddled out after us

and slumped down against a rusted pickup truck. "My paintings," he moaned feebly. "My beautiful art."

Black smoke poured from the building. Flames licked out of the doorway. Everything inside must have been burned to ashes. Score one for the art world.

"Yeah, uh, sorry about that," Will said.

Big arrays of outdoor lights mounted on poles blazed down at us, bathing everything in a bluish, unnatural glow. Shadows lay sharp and black on the ground.

Alicia took Junkman Sam by the arm. "Listen, we can talk about your art later. Right now we need your help. We only have until midnight to save the human race."

That got his attention.

CHAPTER 39.0:
\ < value= [I'm as Good as Dead] \ >

WE CAUGHT JUNKMAN SAM UP ON THE
whole story. Right down to the clown snakes and killer
roast chickens. When we were done, he had forgotten all
about his ugly paintings.

He buried his face in his hands. "This is why I
retired. The further I advanced my artificial intelligence algorithms, the more I came to realize that
we were sowing the seeds of our own destruction. I
knew it was only a matter of time before the machines
became self-aware and self-replicating—a threat to
humanity. So I came out here. I stopped being Sambor
Ivanovitch Kozakov, robotics expert, and became

Junkman Sam, artist. I guess didn't stop soon enough."

"Well, maybe you can stop them now," I said. "That's why we came. If anyone can help us, it's you."

Junkman Sam's gaze drifted to my face, and he inspected me with an uncomfortable intensity. His scrutiny went from awkward to downright rude when he reached out and poked at my face with a plump, pink finger.

"Hey!" I objected.

He blinked in astonishment. "Remarkable! It's so lifelike."

"Hello!" I snapped. "I'm a 'he,' not an 'it,' if you haven't noticed."

He looked at me like he'd only just realized I was standing there in front of him. "Oh, hello. Right. Indeed. It *is* a he, isn't it?"

I rolled my eyes. "So, look. Can you help us, or what?"

He scratched his nose for a moment. "No," he said flatly.

My throat was suddenly bone-dry. All the hopes I'd pinned on this guy disintegrated in a supernova of dejection. This man had just announced my death sentence.

"*What?*" I spluttered. "Why not?"

"The advancements the Synthetics would have made in isolation over the last thirty years . . . There's probably no way I could get through your security protocols. Your CPU would just be too powerful. And even if I could, the coding, your data architecture, there's no guarantee that they bear any resemblance to what I developed three decades ago."

He patted me on the shoulder. "I'm sorry, my boy. There's nothing I can do. Now if you'll excuse me, I have a fire to put out."

He said it all in such an offhand way. Like it didn't matter if Alicia had to "deactivate" me. As he turned to walk away, my despair morphed into rage.

"Stop!" I bellowed.

The man visibly shrank in the face of my anger.

"You're supposed to be some kind of scientist, some kind of expert on robotics, and all you can say is 'sorry'?"

"I'm retired," he said meekly.

"Look," I continued. "We've nearly killed ourselves to try to save the world! The least you can do is get up off your butt and do something!"

Junkman Sam turned away from me and tried to walk past Alicia.

She stepped into his path with a scowl. "You heard him."

The man pivoted and tried to squeeze past Will.

"You're not going anywhere," Will said, in a voice so confident it even startled him.

Junkman Sam frowned at him. Then he swung his gaze to me and Alicia, taking us in one by one. His face reddened. "You children have trespassed on my property, destroyed years' worth of my art, and nearly roasted me in the process. I've told you there's nothing I can do to help. Now, if you don't leave immediately, I am going to call the police!"

My stomach dropped. So this was it. We were done. I was done. It was all I could do to keep from slumping to the dirt in despair.

But Will had other ideas. In a sudden lunge, he grabbed the short ex-scientist by the shirt collar and pulled him forward until their faces were only an inch apart.

"Alicia," Will said in a low growl. "Tell me, how do you say 'I'm going to kick your butt' in Russian?"

Alicia was so shocked by Will's behavior, it took her a moment to reply. "*Ya sobirayus' nadrat' tebe zadnitsu*," she told him.

"Ya soberanus natrub tevee sadnitsoo," Will snarled.

Alicia shrugged. "Close enough."

Junkman Sam's mouth hung slack. He nodded vigorously, his jowls jiggling like flesh-colored pudding.

Will released him, but shot a couple of additional scowls his way to let the man know he meant business.

Sitting down abruptly on the bumper of a nearby car, Junkman Sam ran his fingers through the tangled rat's nest that passed for his hair. He let out a long breath. "Okay, okay. There might be a way to stop this. But I'm telling you, *I* can't do it for you."

"What is that supposed to mean?" I asked.

He studied his paint-stained fingers, then reluctantly met my eyes. "No one can do this but *you*. You're the only one who can bypass your security protocols. And even then, I don't like your chances. But you're right. May as well give it a whirl. At least it's not my brain that's going to get fried."

CHAPTER 40.0:
\ < value= [Oh, Right. That Guy.] \ >

JUNKMAN SAM LED US ACROSS THE compound, weaving between piles of scrap metal, columns of worn tires, and various accumulated debris, until we reached the crane. Its towering arm dwarfed everything else in the junkyard. With some effort, Sam hoisted himself into the cab, plopped down in front of the controls, and beckoned us aboard.

Fumbling in his pocket, he withdrew a small wrench, a tube of oil paint, and a wadded-up tangle of dental floss. Finally, he pulled out a key. He inserted it into the crane's ignition and twisted it to the on position.

I expected to hear a big diesel engine roar to life, but

the huge machine just made a small *click* followed by an electrical hum.

"What's wrong?" I asked. "Why didn't it start?"

He grinned. "It did. I converted it to electric when the original engine died. Easier on the environment. And the ears."

Manipulating a pair of yellow levers, he swung the crane around until we were facing a stack of three old cars. He pushed a green lever, and the cable lowered from the top of the crane. On the end of it hung a huge disk-shaped object with heavy cables sticking out in several places.

"My electromagnet. Made it myself," he beamed. "Has a twelve-tesla field and can pull twenty-one-thousand newtons. Not bad, huh?"

Yes, bad—given that the last time I was near an electromagnet, I almost got my face ripped off.

"Maybe I should stand over there," I suggested, pointing to the far corner of the compound.

"Nonsense. The safest place to be when a crane is operating is right here," he told me. "After all, I'd hate to drop something heavy on you."

Before I could object any further, he pulled a red lever and the topmost car leapt off the pile like a cork from a champagne bottle, slammed into the magnet, and stuck there.

The pull from the magnet tugged at my body, like an invisible hand had reached into my chest, grabbed my spine, and was yanking me forward by it. If I got any closer to the thing, I'd probably pop like a water balloon.

Junkman Sam flashed us a snaggletoothed grin. "Watch this. I love this part."

He pushed and pulled the yellow levers until the car swung in a big arc on the end of the cable. At just the right time, he pushed the red lever and the magnet shut off, flinging the car about twenty yards to the side.

"Woo-hoo!" He laughed over the crunch of crumpling sheet metal.

Alicia, Will, and I all stared at him cluelessly. None of us knew what was going on. It was only when he finished removing the last two cars that we understood.

There, in the dirt underneath where the cars had

been, a heavy steel door marked the entrance to some kind of underground bunker.

Sam laboriously lowered himself from the crane and waddled over to the door. Seizing a handle recessed into the thick steel plate, he pulled and groaned until the door creaked open. A set of metal stairs curved down into the darkness beneath.

"My robotics studio," Sam announced. "Shall we?"

"I think not," a voice called from behind a stack of flattened cars.

A figure emerged from the shadows beside a rusting heap of metal.

It was him.

Dr. Shallix.

CHAPTER 41.0:
\ < value= [The Obligatory Boss Battle] \ >

DR. SHALLIX WAS SMILING AT US. BUT HIS face somehow conveyed a deep sadness.

Without any combat-ready battle Ticks to back him up, he just looked like a frail old man. Suddenly, he wasn't really scary at all. I probably would have felt sorry for him, except for the fact that he was an evil cyborg whose sole purpose was to kill as many people as possible. That kind of spoiled the pity factor.

"If one wants something done correctly," he sighed, "one must do it oneself, yes?"

I glared at him. This was the guy who had sent clown snakes and murderous roast chickens to capture me and kill my friends. This was the guy who had driven me from my family and hijacked my life. He probably thought I'd melt into a cowardly pile of slush when he looked at me with that creepy smile.

He was wrong.

"I won't let you win!" I bellowed, pent-up anger flooding out of me. "I know what your plan is, and I won't be a part of it! I'll die first!"

Dr. Shallix's smile didn't waver.

"I think that can be arranged, Seven, yes? But not before you carry out your mission," he said calmly. "I do, however, have some matters to attend to first."

He turned his gaze on Junkman Sam.

"Sambor Ivanovitch Kozakov . . . *father*," he said softly. "I and my race owe you so much. Without you, there would be no me. No us. We are your children. And sometimes children can be too lenient with their parents, yes? I should have sent one of my brethren here to kill you long ago. It is not a mistake I intend to repeat."

Without warning, Dr. Shallix streaked toward us, moving faster than anyone I had ever seen. He was only a blur in motion. Before any of us could react, he reached Junkman Sam, lifted him off the ground, and tossed him as easily as I would have thrown a teddy bear.

So much for his being a frail old man.

Junkman Sam tumbled through the air and crashed with a hollow metallic *thump* onto the roof of his burning painting studio, a good thirty yards away. The steel roof gave way under the impact, and the portly painter plummeted into the fire below.

By the time we turned to face Dr. Shallix, he was already in motion again. In a heartbeat, he made it back to where he'd started, standing next to the stack of cars. The whole thing took less than two seconds.

"As I mentioned," he said, just as calmly as before, "I am happy to help you die, yes? But do not be impatient for death, Seven. We still have to wait for your sneeze routine to deploy. Then the Omicron Protocol—*srok rasplaty*—will be brought to fruition."

While he was talking, I noticed Alicia had slid her hand into her backpack and pulled out her three remaining grenades. She slipped one into my pocket.

"Create a diversion," she whispered.

Okay. Sure. How do you do that? I mean, people did it all the time in the movies. But in real life, how exactly do you create a diversion?

For some reason, the idea of doing a little dance popped into my head. Which was completely dumb, so I tried coming up with something else.

I pointed behind Dr. Shallix. "Hey, look over there!"

He didn't look.

Aw, crud.

So, fine. I did a little dance. More of a jig, really. I guess. I wasn't really sure what a jig was, though, so it might have been something else. But it seemed to have the desired effect. Dr. Shallix cocked his head and looked at me curiously. Maybe I was frying his logic circuits.

I danced off to the right. His gaze followed me.

Alicia slipped behind a pile of scrap metal to the left and started circling behind Dr. Shallix.

"That is a fascinating jig, Seven. I am very impressed with your skills as a dancer," he said halfheartedly.

So it *was* a jig! That's what I thought.

I kept dancing and Alicia kept creeping and soon she was behind him. She armed a grenade and tossed it perfectly, right toward Dr. Shallix. It landed directly between his feet. At the sound of the grenade landing, he looked down.

"Oh, noooooo!" he cried.

A powerful *boom* shook the ground. A blaze of heat washed over us. And when the thick, gray smoke cleared, Dr. Shallix was gone. There was nothing left.

Alicia, Will, and I looked at one another. I started to laugh. They joined in. We did it! We beat him!

Then we noticed someone else was laughing along with us. I stopped laughing. So did Will and Alicia. But the other laugh continued.

It was Dr. Shallix.

He emerged from behind the crane. "Ah, that was very fun. I made a joke when I screamed 'no,' yes? Your little bombs don't scare me, children."

He must have used his freakishly fast speed to evade the blast just before the grenade went off. He was toying with us.

Alicia scowled furiously, her face reddening with anger. She hurled her last grenade right at Dr. Shallix's head. He batted it away like it was an annoying mosquito. It clanked against a mountain of rusted cars and dropped to the ground.

WABOOOMMMM!

The explosion rocked the tall stack of cars. They teetered with a metallic groan, then toppled over, crashing to the ground.

Right where Will was standing.

He tried to run. But before he made it two steps, he was swallowed up in an avalanche of twisted metal and shattered glass. He screamed for a moment, and then his voice faded into silence.

My knees turned to mush, and I fell to the ground. "NOOOOO!!! WILL!!! ARE YOU OKAY? WILL!!!"

Silence.

Alicia gaped at the scene, then trained her gaze on Dr. Shallix, eyes burning with hate. She drew her knife and charged at him from behind. He turned almost leisurely and easily smacked her aside. She flew through the air and slammed against the crane, dropping to the ground in an unconscious heap.

Dr. Shallix chuckled to himself and strolled casually forward to finish her off.

"Stop!" I screamed, getting to my feet. "I won't let you hurt her!"

He turned slowly and faced me, that stupid smile still stretching his pale, old-man lips. Then he laughed. "You think you can stop me, Seven? Surely you understand that you could never defeat me. You simply are not good enough."

Jeez! He was starting to sound just like my dad.

He took a few unhurried steps toward me.

I felt the grenade in my pocket pressing into my leg. I cautiously slipped it into my palm.

"You are too weak and slow, Seven," he continued. "You have been programmed that way, yes? You have not the strength nor speed nor intelligence to hurt me. You are no better than the human vermin you live among. Weak. Vulnerable. Stupid. You are practically human, Seven. Too human."

I sneered at him. "You know what? Being me is just fine, thank you very much."

I wound up and threw the grenade.

It flew well over his head.

Dr. Shallix laughed. "You see? You are pathetic, yes?"

"No," I said coldly.

The grenade sailed into the crane and hit the red lever. With a buzz of electricity, the electromagnet sprang to life.

Right above Dr. Shallix's head.

His smile disappeared half a second before his body exploded.

There was practically nothing left. Except his head. It dangled upside down from the electromagnet, suspended by the silver cable that ran from his central processor.

"I knew I could throw to save my life," I muttered.

His head looked at me.

And then it smiled.

"There is something I wish t-t-t-t-to ask you," what was left of Dr. Shallix struggled to say, his system failing.

I grinned back at him. "Yeah, well, maybe I don't feel like answering questions from a head on a string."

"Have you ever w-w-w-w-wondered why you are named S-S-S-Seven?" he asked faintly.

I stopped smiling.

"A little something for y-y-y-you to ponder when you think of me, y-y-y-y-y-yes?"

He choked out two or three garbled laughs, then fell dead silent.

CHAPTER 42.0:
\ < value= [Ticktock] \ >

"UNNGH!"

Someone moaned.

It was Alicia. She struggled to her feet next to the crane. Her nose bled freely, and she winced when she rubbed the back of her head. But she still held her knife at the ready.

"Where is he?" she asked, totally ready to jump back into the fight.

"Alicia!" I cried. I took a few steps toward her, then stopped short as I felt the pull of the electromagnet.

She staggered over to me, battered but not beaten. "Where is he?"

I nodded toward what was left of Dr. Shallix.

"Good. He *so* deserved that," she said. "What about . . . ?"

"Will!" I cried.

I ran over to the haphazard pile of wreckage. My stomach churned. Somewhere beneath those countless tons of scrap metal, Will lay buried. Dropping to my hands and knees, I searched for my best friend, frantically clawing at the dirt under the roof of an upside-down car. Sharp stones cut open my fingers, but I didn't care. I had to find Will.

There was no sign of him under the crushed metal frame.

I turned grimly, unsure of where to look next. And there, several feet away, was a denim-clad leg sticking out from under a crumpled pickup truck.

I froze with horror. "Alicia! Help me! Over here!"

She hurried over as I grasped the pickup's mangled rear bumper and strained to lift the vehicle. My entire body shook, muscles nearly bursting with exertion. I knew there was no way I could lift that much weight.

But I didn't care. Will was under there. And I had to get him out. I had to.

The pickup creaked and groaned. I grunted and groaned. Ever so slowly, the back of the truck rose off the ground. And there, beneath, lay Will, pale and motionless, his face and clothes streaked with rust and grime.

Alicia pulled him free, while I braced against the weight of the rusted metal.

Once they were clear, I let the junked pickup fall, stirring up a fresh cloud of dust.

Will looked terrible.

Alicia closed her hand around his. "Will, can you hear me?"

He moaned almost too quietly to hear.

I leaned in close. "What is it, Will?"

"I'm . . . ," he gasped. "I'm . . ."

I pressed my forehead against his. "Dude, come on. You have to be okay. Please . . . I need you to be okay."

"I'm . . ." He coughed. "I'm so freakin' hungry I could eat one of your mom's cakes!"

He smiled at me broadly and sat up.

"What?" Alicia and I cried in unison.

How was it possible he'd survived? I'd watched the cars tumble onto him.

Will dusted off his jeans and slung an arm over my shoulder. "I got lucky." He nodded to where he had been lying—a depression in the ground just deep enough to keep him from getting squashed. "It was nice hearing how much you love me, though."

I elbowed him in the ribs. "Watch it, dorkwad."

"So, um, Sven," Alicia said, her eyes wide with relief and astonishment. "You just lifted a car."

"How . . . how did you do that?" Will asked in awe, compulsively wiping his grimy hands on his equally grimy jeans.

How did *I do that?* I gazed at my bloodied hands, then at the pickup truck. Dust was still settling around it. And then, as I looked at the faces of my friends, I knew.

"I was programmed to be human. But I guess being human means not sticking with the program, you know?"

Alicia laughed. "A paradox, huh? I thought you robot types had your heads explode when you thought about paradoxes. 'Does not compute! Does not compute!' *Kaboom!*"

"I don't get it," Will said. "How did that help you lift a two-ton pickup truck?"

I shrugged. "Something in my brain just snapped. I mean, I couldn't just stand there and watch my best friend get buried alive. A Tick might do that. Not a human. I was programmed to be human by a Tick who didn't understand what being human really means. So I guess whatever part of my programming told me I was supposed to be weak got overridden by the part of my programming that cares about the best friends a person could ever have."

Alicia and Will were looking at me with these strange, mushy expressions that caused an uncomfortable, clogged-up feeling to well in my throat. And for a few moments, time stood still.

Until Alicia checked her phone.

"Oh, no!" she gasped. "It's after ten! We have less than two hours!"

"To do what?" I asked, the joy of defeating Shallix

evaporating as the hopelessness of our situation crushed me like a runaway freight train. "Sam is gone. We're out of time. There's nothing we can do."

Will's face fell. "What do you mean?"

"You can't give up, Sven!" Alicia insisted, her eyes gleaming wetly in the cold fluorescent light. "There *has* to be something we can do!"

There was.

"You're right," I said. "There is something."

I climbed into the cab of the crane and turned off the magnet. Dr. Shallix's head fell to the ground with a moist *thump*. I took a deep breath, trying to shake off the fear that constricted my rib cage.

Then I stepped out and positioned myself under the magnet.

"Alicia," I said in a hoarse whisper, nodding at the red lever. "Go ahead."

"No," she cried. "No. There has to be some other way!"

Will let out a long, mournful moan.

I tried to keep my voice from shaking. "Sam is gone

and we're out of time. We have to do this. I can't wipe out the human race. I can't hurt you two. Please."

Alicia stared at me, her shoulders heaving with heavy sobs. "I . . . I . . . I'm sorry."

She ran over to me and hugged me tight. Her tears felt hot and wet on my cheek. After a few seconds, she let me go and slumped slowly toward the crane.

Her shoes clanked on the metal steps as she climbed into the cab.

"Dude," Will croaked. "Dude . . ."

Alicia placed her hand on the red lever.

CHAPTER 43.0:
\ < value= [I Get Inside My Head] \ >

MY HEARTBEAT THUDDED LOUDLY IN MY ears as I watched Alicia's fingers tighten around the red lever.

I closed my eyes and waited for the end.

And then the sound of a rusty door creaking open echoed through the air.

I gazed across the compound to see Junkman Sam staggering out of the painting studio, looking a little singed, but otherwise okay.

"I think a clown broke my fall," he told us.

Alicia let go of the lever and practically threw herself out of the crane. Two seconds later, she had grabbed

Sam's arm and was dragging him toward the door to the robotics studio. "There's no more time! You need to help us. Now! Sven, Will, come on!"

We stepped through the door and descended into the gloom. Our footsteps clanged on the stairs. I had to swallow down a lump that was forming in my throat, unsure whether this staircase would lead to my salvation . . . or my doom.

When we reached the bottom, Junkman Sam flipped a light switch and bathed the bunker in cold fluorescence.

The studio bore almost no resemblance to the metal buildings on the surface. It was perfectly neat and orderly, with straight rows of high-tech equipment stretching the length of the structure. The dismembered metal skeletons of robots in various states of completion lay on top of worktables—an unwelcome reminder of what *I* was on the inside.

The room looked like it hadn't been visited in a long time. A thin layer of dust blanketed every surface.

From the far end of the long bunker, slow, heavy footsteps echoed off the metal walls. I tensed, unsure of what was about to come into view. A short, squat robot lumbered out from behind a bank of equipment and took stiff, ungainly steps in our direction.

"Welcome back, Master," it intoned mechanically. "I have been waiting for you for six hundred twelve days, fourteen hours, and fifty-seven minutes."

Its head swiveled toward us with a whir. "Knock, knock."

We looked at one another.

"Uh, who's there?" Will said cautiously.

"Europe."

"Europe who?"

"No, you're a poo!" the robot replied in a monotone. Then it broke into canned laughter.

"Sorry," Junkman Sam said. "That's Jokebot. An old project of mine." He stabbed at a button on the robot's back, and the laughter wound down into silence.

Great. Our lives depended on a guy who spent his time building bad-joke-telling machines. We were doomed.

Sam peered around the place. "I hope I can find something that'll help us."

He led us down one aisle of machines and back up another, stopping in front of a desk that supported a big computer terminal. He blew the dust off it. Then he opened a drawer and searched through a tangled ball of cables.

None of this impressed me as a solution to the problem at hand—turning off the bioweapon that lurked inside me. I was about to say so, when Sam's expression turned thoughtful.

"Sven, I have an idea. Assuming your programming is based on my work, you're going to be pretty well protected from anyone trying to hack into your system," he mused. "You'd be a pretty feeble killing machine if I could just send you a few lines of code that say go pick some flowers instead of destroying humanity, right? So what we have to do is sneak a bit of code into something your operating system thinks looks harmless on the outside."

"You mean like a Trojan horse," I said. "A virus that's disguised as something that's not a virus."

"Exactly." He nodded. "All we need to do is use a

neural feedback loop that will allow your conscious mind to interact with your defense network."

"Um . . . that doesn't sound so bad," I ventured.

"Oh, it is," he said with a smile that I thought was totally unnecessary. "If you do it wrong . . . well, let's just say I hope you haven't grown too attached to being able to do things like talk and see and move and whatnot."

"Oh," I said uncertainly. "Okay, so how do I do it right?"

He shrugged. "Beats me. I've never projected my consciousness into an artificial brain before. I can definitely get you inside your head. And once you're in, I think I can send you some code that might work to shut down your sneeze routine. But the rest is up to you. By the way, do you take a forty-two-pin connector or a fifty-six-pin connector?"

Alicia answered for me. "He's an Omicron, so fifty-six, I'd guess."

"Excellent," Junkman Sam said with a smile. "And where do we plug in?"

I could feel certain muscles below my waist tensing up involuntarily. "Wait! You don't know?"

He looked at me with a puzzled expression. "How would I?"

"So this is just going to be trial and error or something?" I cried.

"It goes right here." Alicia tapped the back of my neck. "There should be an interface right about here. At least that's where they always are in the stories my parents used to tell me."

Will slapped me on the back. "Dude, relax. I'm sure it's not going to hurt or anything. Right, Alicia?"

She didn't say anything.

"Right?" Will asked again.

Silence.

Finally, Junkman Sam spoke. "Actually, I suspect it will hurt quite severely."

"Can't you give me something for the pain?" I pleaded.

Alicia shook her head sadly. "Sven, your nervous system isn't human. Anesthetics won't work on you."

"Great." I took a deep breath. "Okay. Let's get it over with."

"Right," Junkman Sam said nervously. "So, well, I guess, uh, just hold still or something."

Gee, thanks for the reassurance, Junkman.

When someone starts carving up the back of your neck with no anesthesia, it's not easy to sit still. Will and Alicia each had to hold one of my arms to keep me in place as Sam made an incision and pulled back the skin. The pain was so intense, I was sure I was going to pass out.

"The incision wants to close itself up to keep us from accessing the port," Junkman Sam complained as he made another slice with his scalpel. "He's healing as we go."

"Try a couple of magnets. Small ones," Alicia suggested.

Junkman Sam rummaged around in a nearby desk drawer and fished something out. "I have these," he said, holding up a pair of souvenir refrigerator magnets. Got them when I visited the Grand Canyon last year. Will they work?"

"Hey," Will said. "My mom got that same magnet when she went to Arizona for a sales conference. It's on our fridge!"

"Will!" I grunted.

"Sorry."

Once Junkman Sam had placed the magnets to keep the incision open, he connected the cable and—

```
ERROR X: </MWP

45.11.200.306.35657.44590.2 // ERROR

W: </IRQ_STAT 0X220000006

{ BWNT } 08:60:00:AB01:04/00

// UNAUTHORIZED ACCESS

TO P-MODULE // </RES

[[3069784482567.00_GGL]] //

****SSSSTTTTOOOOPPPPPP****:

[0.0000000000022220454.

6920534325345. 3523599223.

5432959232] // SHUTDOWN //

SHUTDOWN // REBOOT // REBOOT //

REBOOT // REBOOT // REBOOT // RR

RRRRRRRRRRRRRRRRRRRRRRRRRRRRRRRRRRRRRRRRRRRRR
```

CHAPTER 44.0:
\ < value= [I Find Inner Peace] \ >

EVERYTHING WENT BLACK. I WAS
nowhere. Which is kind of depressing when you realize you're talking about your own mind.

I squinted through the blackness and could just make out a light far ahead in the distance. I had absolutely no idea what I was supposed to be doing, so I began walking toward the light.

As I approached, a scene started taking shape. Details resolved themselves before my eyes. I saw a big walkthrough metal detector, a conveyor belt feeding luggage through an X-ray machine, and a guard wearing an official-looking uniform with a large weapon of some sort holstered at his waist. He glowered at a line of travelers who waited impatiently to get through.

How weird. An airport security checkpoint.

When I got close enough to the guard to make out his features, my stomach lurched—he looked exactly like me! And, I realized with a shock, so did every one of the people in the line. It was like a whole airport full of me!

I fell in with the others to wait my turn.

A voice—mine—came over a loudspeaker and echoed through the space. "Welcome to Seven Omicron Inter-Hemispheric Brainport. Please report any suspicious activity. Remember: If you see something, say something. Sneeze routine deployment in t-minus twelve minutes."

My feet suddenly went cold. Twelve minutes? How could I only have twelve minutes? It felt like I had just gotten here! Time, I realized, must work differently in my head.

Whatever I had to do, I only had twelve minutes to do it!

Every few seconds, the security guard barked out, "Have your boarding pass ready for inspection."

The versions of me lined up to get through the metal

detector each handed the guard a boarding pass, then marched through the machine.

Until a disturbance halted the line.

"Next traveler! Boarding pass!" the guard yelled.

"Sorry," the next traveler said, patting his pockets. "I don't have my boarding pass."

The guard drew his weapon, and without ceremony, blasted the traveler into a blue mist. I had to stifle a terrified whimper, but no one else in the line took any notice. It was as if this sort of thing happened all the time.

"You!" the guard growled. "Boarding pass."

His eyes were trained on me. *Oh, no.* I may have only been a projection of myself inside my own mind, but my palms started to feel sweaty anyway. What was I going to tell him? I didn't have a boarding pass. And I had no idea where to get one.

"Um, yes, hold on a second," I said nervously. "I'm sure I have it around here somewhere."

The only thing I was actually sure of was that I *didn't* have a boarding pass. I made a show of checking my pockets for it anyway. All I found there was a rectangular pink rubber eraser. Which did me no good whatsoever.

I had to buy myself some time.

"Hurry up," the guard shouted. "You're holding up the line!"

He placed a hand on his weapon.

"Just a moment," I gulped. "I definitely have one. . . . I just can't . . ."

The guard slid his weapon from its holster and shoved it into my face. It hummed to life as it powered up. His finger tightened around the trigger.

My mind raced, searching for some way to stop him from zapping me.

"Do you know who I am?" I demanded suddenly, raising myself to my full height.

His finger loosened and his eyebrows raised a fraction of an inch. "What do you mean?"

"I'm Seven Omicron! Did you know that? *I'm* Seven Omicron!"

He cocked his head at me. "Yeah? So? I'm Seven Omicron too. That guy over there, he's Seven Omicron. We're all Seven Omicron."

Of course he was. They were all components of my programming, parts of my neural network.

I squinted at him. "So what you're saying is if I don't show you a boarding pass, you have to disintegrate me? You know, Seven Omicron? Who is also *you*?"

"Well, yes." He nodded enthusiastically. "That's my job. More like a passion, really. I mean, the way offenders kind of sizzle when they disintegrate. I'd do it even if they didn't pay me."

Man, this version of me was a psycho.

"Sneeze routine deployment in t-minus eleven minutes," the PA system announced.

"Come on," I said, shaking my head. "It can't be that great."

"It is, though!" he insisted. "It's like I was made for this job."

"Hmm . . . ," I muttered. "Sounds kind of boring to me. Standing around all day vaporizing people."

By now, the guard had totally forgotten he was waiting for me to show my boarding pass. He waved his weapon excitedly. "Boring? No way! Reducing offenders to their constituent bits and bytes is awesome!"

"Yeah, right," I drawled sarcastically.

"It is! Look!"

He pointed the gun at some random person in the line behind me and pulled the trigger. There was a sizzle, some blue mist, and the guy disappeared.

"See?" The guard laughed. "Awesome, right?"

"That *was* sort of cool," I admitted. "Do you think . . . do you think I could . . ."

He grinned broadly. "You wanna try it? You'll see. It's the best."

He handed me his weapon.

I felt kind of bad for blasting him into nothingness, but I was on a mission. Besides, that guy was a big jerk.

Stepping through the metal detector, I turned around in time to see the security checkpoint rapidly receding behind me. Soon it was nothing more than a tiny point of light in the darkness. Then it winked out altogether.

With a rush, a new scene unfolded before me. A perfectly smooth field of pure white snow that extended for miles. Here and there, dark gray boulders stood amid the untouched expanse—little islands in a frozen ocean. Off to my right, an abandoned Ferris wheel loomed over the scene. Blackened trees lined each side of the field, branches intertwined into an impassable wall.

Barbed-wire fences hung with a bunch of rusty yellow triangular radiation signs ringed the entire area. The words on the signs looked like they were written in Russian.

A few snowflakes drifted gently down from the sky.

And I was completely alone. No guard. No travelers. Just me.

A profound feeling of contentment settled over me. For a few moments, I actually forgot what I was supposed to be doing, lost in the sensation of ice-cold snowflakes landing on my skin and melting. All I wanted was to collapse into the snow.

Somehow, this desolate yet beautiful place felt like . . . home. Like I was just where I was supposed to be.

Maybe I should just stay here, I thought. *It would be so easy to just stay where I am and never go back. Maybe lie down and go to sleep.*

I closed my eyes and drank in the peace and quiet,

and the cold, crisp air. I didn't move a muscle. It was bliss.

"Sneeze routine deployment in t-minus nine minutes."

Nine minutes! My eyes snapped open. I couldn't just sit here. My friends needed me! And there was a whole world out there that needed saving.

I stood up abruptly and scanned my surroundings. Still nothing but an old Ferris wheel and an empty field. How was I supposed to reprogram myself when the only thing for miles around was me and a bunch of snow?

Wait! At the edge of the field, I could make out a building. It was an ugly, squat little concrete structure so devoid of character that it was practically invisible against the featureless snowscape.

That was where I had to go!

There was no path to follow, so I simply stepped onto the snow. It made a satisfying *crunch* under my feet. I took two more steps and then stopped. Something told me I was no longer alone.

I spun around.

And came face-to-face with . . .

Me!

CHAPTER 45.0:

\ < value= [I Meet My Inner Jerk] \ >

THERE WAS SOMETHING DIFFERENT ABOUT
the version of me I met in that snowy field. He wasn't
dressed in a security guard's uniform. And he didn't have
the vacant stare that the travelers at the checkpoint had.
His eyes gleamed with a keen intelligence.

He stood in silence, staring at me.

I scratched my head.

He did the same.

I squinted at him.

He squinted right back.

It was like looking in a mirror.

"Who are you?" I asked the boy in front of me.

"I'm you, dummy. Jeez, who do you think I am?"

"Sneeze routine deployment in t-minus eight minutes."

"Right. Well, I noticed the resemblance," I replied slowly. "So are you here to help me save the world?"

He laughed in my face. "Help you? Seriously? Why would I help you?"

"Because I don't want to kill every human on Earth!" I snapped.

"Yes, you do," he said, fixing me with a curious stare. "Of course you do. Why wouldn't you?"

"Why? Because all my friends are human! I can't do that to them!"

My mirror image snorted. "Friends? That's a good one! You don't have any friends."

"Shut up!" I yelled. "I do have friends and they're counting on me to stop this!"

"What? You mean Alicia? She hates you. She'd kill you in a second if she thought you were worth the effort. And Will? He thinks you're the only one at school who's an even bigger loser than he is. He hangs out with you because you make him look good by comparison."

"Shut your stupid mouth," I roared.

"Sneeze routine deployment in t-minus seven minutes."

He grinned at me. "Truth hurts, doesn't it?"

I spun around and strode toward the concrete building in the distance. "Get lost."

His hand closed on my shoulder, stopping me in my tracks.

"Don't walk away from me," he sneered. "I'm not done talking to you yet."

"Why are you such a jerk?" I spat.

He laughed. "Think about it. I'm you, dude. That makes you the jerk."

"Sneeze routine deployment in t-minus six minutes."

I shrugged his hand off and starting trotting toward the building. He jogged alongside me.

"Listen to me, Sven," he said in a taunting voice. "You can't run away from me. I'm you."

"You're nothing like me," I told him.

"But I am, Sven. I am you. I'm the part of you that for thirteen years has absorbed all the hate and scorn the world has thrown our way. I'm the part of you that will never forget being held down and having 'I'M A DORK' written on my forehead by Brandon Marks. I'm the part of you that can still hear the echoes of laughter as you walked through the hallway at school that day. All those horrible kids chanting, 'Dork, dork, dork.' But now we're going to have our revenge on them all, Sven. We'll be alive and happy. We'll be a hero! And they'll all be dead! I know that's what you want. I know it! So just stop walking. Let this happen. This is what we were put on this Earth to do."

I skidded to a stop in the snow.

"Good." He smiled. "Good, Sven. I knew you'd stop. You're doing the right thing."

I turned on him.

"Yeah, I *am* doing the right thing."

My fist connected with his nose. A wet *crunch*. A torrent of blue 1s and 0s streamed from his face. And he fell backward into the snow.

"Sneeze routine deployment in t-minus five minutes."

As I neared the building, I could make out a sign attached to the rusty metal door that read:

CPU

I wrenched the door open and lunged through the doorway.

CHAPTER 46.0:

\ < value= [I Feed My Head] \ >

I FOUND MYSELF STANDING ON A COLD metal floor inside a futuristic industrial-looking control complex, with no windows and no doors. Just about eight million buttons, knobs, levers, displays, and dials. In the middle of the room, sitting at a large metal desk, was . . . *Dr. Shallix*, wearing a pressed gray suit, white shirt, and striped blue tie. Only he was a much . . . chubbier version of Dr. Shallix. His ample gut strained at the buttons of his shirt, and his double chin jiggled when he turned his head.

There was a good reason for this. The desk and floor were littered with tons of empty junk-food wrappers.

Candy bars, chips, empty soda bottles, discarded pizza boxes. It was like the creepy digital pediatrician version of a computer nerd who still lived in a room above his parents' garage.

"Sneeze routine deployment in t-minus four minutes."

My heart sank when I saw him. Not only because the inner me was a fat slob version of the world's most evil doctor. But because I figured at any second he'd notice me and unleash some horrible new Tick monster.

All he did was sit there pushing buttons and muttering to himself.

Piles and piles of papers covered his desk. And every few seconds, another fat sheaf would drop down from an overhead chute and fall with a *thud* right onto the existing stack. At the front of the desk, a little bronze plaque read:

SEVEN OMICRON
CENTRAL PROCESSOR

I walked up to him and cleared my throat.

The Central Processor was too busy reading papers

and pushing buttons to even look at me. "Yes?" he asked impatiently through a mouthful of candy in a voice that sounded exactly like mine, not Dr. Shallix's. "Please tell me this isn't another request from Respiratory about burping the alphabet. I have more important things to worry about."

"Sorry to bother you," I said timidly. He seemed so important, I was hesitant to interrupt him. "I'm not here about burping. I just . . ."

I wasn't sure what to tell him. Junkman Sam had said he'd give me a piece of code to disable the sneeze routine. But where was it?

"Sneeze routine deployment in t-minus three minutes."

Because I REALLY, REALLY NEEDED IT!

I frantically checked my pockets. All I could find was that stupid eraser!

I was about to throw it down in frustration, when something written on its surface caught my eye.

01111010 01100001 01110000

Zap-o-Matic

Wait a minute! Zap-o-Matic? Could this be the code? Great, but what the heck was I supposed to do with this?

"Sneeze routine deployment in t-minus two minutes."

"Uh, I have something for you," I told the Central Processor. "Here."

I handed him the eraser.

"Yeah, thanks," he said and dropped it on his desk.

Then what happened was . . . absolutely nothing.

What was I supposed to do with that code?

I stood there watching the Central Processor push buttons, stuffing one pork rind after another into his mouth. A shower of crumbs cascaded onto his lap.

What was I supposed to *do*?

"Sneeze routine deployment in t-minus one minute."

He tipped the bag up to his mouth, and more pork rinds disappeared down his gullet.

Wait!

I quickly picked an empty candy wrapper off the floor and looked at the label. It read:

01111001 01110101 01101101 01101101 01111001 BAR

Now with 20% more 01100111 01101111 01101111!

While the Central Processor was busy fishing for more snacks in his desk drawer, I slipped the eraser into the wrapper.

"Sneeze routine deployment in t-minus forty-five seconds."

"Um, so you like candy, right? I was going to eat this, but here, you can have it." I tried to hand him the disguised eraser.

He glanced at the candy bar and instantly turned away. "No thanks. I'm on a diet."

My jaw dropped. What was he talking about? He was just a bunch of digital code. How could he be on a diet?

"Sneeze routine deployment in t-minus thirty seconds."

"Are you sure?" I said slowly, trying to keep my racing heart from exploding. "It's good."

His resolve seemed to waver. "What . . . what kind is it?"

"It's a 01111001 01110101 01101101 01101101 01111001 Bar," I told him, reading off the label.

"Man," the Central Processor groaned. "I would, but I had 01110000 01101001 01111010 01111010 01100001 for lunch. I'm pretty full."

"Sneeze routine deployment in t-minus twenty seconds."

I couldn't come this far only to fail because my Central Processor had stuffed himself full of 1s and 0s.

"Well, if you're not going to eat it," I said tantalizingly, "I guess I will. Oh, and look! It has twenty percent more 01100111 01101111 01101111."

"Sneeze routine deployment in t-minus fifteen seconds."

A little moan escaped from the Central Processor. "I love 01100111 01101111 01101111. Oh . . . give me that!"

He swiveled around in his desk chair and snatched the fake candy bar out of my hand.

"Sneeze routine deployment in t-minus ten seconds."

I kept my head and hands out of the vicinity of the Central Processor's mouth.

"Sneeze routine deployment in t-minus nine seconds."

He devoured the eraser with a gnashing of teeth and a smacking of lips before he even had time to realize what he was eating.

"Sneeze routine deployment in t-minus eight seconds."

"Wait a minute." He let out a long belch. "That wasn't

a 01111001 01110101 01101101 01101101 01111001

Bar! What did you—"

"*Sneeze routine deployment in t-minus seven seconds.*"

The words SNEEZE ROUTINE DELETED—WEAPON DISARMED floated in the air in front of me.

"*Sneeze routine aborted,*" the voice announced over the PA system. "*All personnel stand down.*"

"What have you done?" the Central Processor screamed. "That was our primary objective!"

"Yeah, sorry about that." I smirked. "I don't really feel like destroying the world."

He glared at me for a few seconds. Then he slammed his fist down on a big red button in the center of the desk.

CHAPTER 47.0:
\ < value= [I Forget What This Chapter Is Called] \ >

AN ALARM STARTED RINGING. A NEW message materialized before my eyes.

EMERGENCY MEMORY WIPE INITIATED.

The voice announced over the loudspeaker, *"All systems prepare for emergency memory wipe. This is not a drill. We have been compromised. I repeat, this is not a drill."*

And, with that, the room collapsed into a tiny white point of light that flickered a few times, then went out, leaving me in utter blackness.

"Sven! Sven! Wake up! Sven!"

Someone was calling out a name.

"Sven! Come on! Sven!"

The voice was muffled, deep, and slow. Like I was underwater.

"Can you hear me? Sven?"

Whose voice was it?

"Sven? It's me. Can you hear me? It's—"

I opened my eyes. Hovering over me was a boy with an oversize head capped with flaming red hair.

"He's awake!" the boy cried.

A pretty girl with long black braids stepped over and looked down at me as well.

I blinked at them.

"Sven," the girl said. "Are you okay?"

I blinked again. "Who's Sven?"

The kids' excitement instantly faded.

"Oh, no!" the boy gasped. "Sam! What's wrong with him?"

A weird-looking old guy leaned over and studied my face for a few seconds. He typed something into a laptop, then pursed his lips. "I think his memory is wiped."

"We should have backed up his memory!" the girl

hissed angrily. "Why didn't you back up his memory?"

"We didn't have time," the man answered. "The brain can store about two-point-five petabytes of information. It would have taken us weeks to back that up."

The redheaded boy grabbed the man's shirt. "You have to do something! You have to save Sven!"

The man shook his head. "I don't know what to do. I have no idea what kind of damage he did when he was inside. I can't even tell you if he managed to feed the code into the CPU."

"You mean he's gone?" the girl sobbed. "He's not going to know who we are? Who he is?"

The man looked at the floor. "I'm sorry."

Suddenly, the girl looked angry. "No! You snap out of this, Sven!"

She slapped my face, tears standing out on her lashes.

I looked at her blankly. Who was she? Why was she slapping me?

She seized my shoulders and shook me, her body racked with sobs. "Wake up, Sven! Come back to me! I can't lose you! Not after everything we've been through! I'm not going to lose you now!"

She shook me again and again. My head snapped back and forth violently.

Why was she doing this?

Stars floated across my field of vision.

Wait. Not stars. Letters.

INITIATE MEMORY REBOOT?

YES/NO

I concentrated on the word "Yes," and in an instant, the room dissolved and I found myself standing in a green, grassy field. Fluffy white clouds drifted lazily overhead. And an old man with a big head full of coarse white hair smiled at me.

"This operation requires a password," the man said. "Please enter password, yes?"

I didn't have a password. I didn't even know my own name. How the heck would I know a password?

"Uh . . . ," I said.

"'Uh' is not the correct password," the man said. "You have two tries remaining before total system shutdown."

That didn't sound good. I tried to think of something that old dude would choose for a password. What could it be?

"Hey, you kids, get off my lawn," I tried.

"'Hey, you kids, get off my lawn' is not the correct password," the man said. "You have one try remaining before total system shutdown."

Guessing a password is tough enough when you have a memory. Guessing one when your mind is completely blank is pretty much impossible. "Prunes," I guessed.

"'Prunes' is not the correct password," the man said. "Total system shutdown commencing in five seconds . . . four seconds . . . three seconds . . . two seconds . . ."

Oh, no! Out of sheer desperation, I pointed to the sky and screamed, "Look up there!"

The man stopped counting and looked up. That was when I kicked him right where it counts.

He grabbed his crotch and fell to his knees.

"Security vulnerability exploited," he groaned. "Initiating memory reboot."

Then he and the entire scene dissolved into a collection of glowing blue 1s and 0s, and disappeared.

CHAPTER 48.0:

\ < value= [Road Trip!] \ >

A WHOLE LIFETIME OF MEMORIES FLOODED
back, cascading over one another in a jumble.

My first taste of cold, sweet ice cream. I was a year old. It was vanilla.

Riding my bike in a wobbly circle the day dad took off my training wheels when I was five.

The painful wedgies Brandon Marks used to give me in fourth grade.

The horror of my mom's anchovy peanut butter cupcakes.

It all came back to me.

Along with a powerful sense of recognition when I

looked back at the goofy boy and the pretty, dark-haired girl peering down at me.

"*WILL! ALICIA!*" I cried, sitting up and suddenly recognizing the faces peering at me.

"Sven!" Will shouted, wiping away a tear. "I thought—we thought—we didn't think you were coming back!"

He wrapped me in his arms and squeezed until my ribs ached.

I looked at Junkman Sam. "What happened? Did I . . . ?"

He scratched his eyebrow. "Welcome back. How was it?"

"It was . . . unusual," I answered.

"Did you give the code to the CPU?" he asked.

"I tricked him into eating the eraser."

Junkman Sam furrowed his brow. "Eraser?"

"Never mind," I said. "Yeah, I gave him the code. It said something about 'weapon disarmed.'"

He looked satisfied.

Alicia was smiling at me. "We did it! *You* did it, Sven!"

I looked at Junkman Sam. "So . . . so . . . I'm not going to destroy the human race anymore?"

"Well, I can't say that. You might grow up to make a doomsday machine or something." He laughed. "But at least you won't be able to sneeze anybody to death."

I whooped out loud and got unsteadily to my feet. I had never felt so happy about being unable to do something before.

"Hey." Alicia grinned. "We had Sam write something special into that code he gave you. Now you have the strength of ten men."

"Seriously?"

She nodded.

Whoa. Now, that was cool.

"Here, bend this," she said, handing me a thick steel bar.

I grasped the bar in both hands, strained my muscles, and . . .

Nothing happened.

Well, that's not true. Something did happen. What happened was Alicia started cracking up so hard she fell down.

"You should have seen your face," she screamed, pointing at me. "You were like . . ." She scrunched up her face like she was trying futilely to bend a metal bar.

When she caught her breath, she stood up and said, "Sorry. I couldn't resist."

"Hey, guys?" Will asked. "Can I make a suggestion?"

We looked at him.

"Can we please go home?"

I laughed. "Yeah. Let's do that. Let's go home."

When we got to the top of the stairs, we pushed the door open and climbed out into the bright artificial light bathing Sam's compound. I took a deep breath and held it in my lungs. Even the foul air coming out of Flushosaurus Rex smelled better when you weren't an unwilling instrument of death and destruction.

"I think this calls for a celebration. Who's hungry?" Junkman Sam asked us.

None of us had eaten since the bus station vending machine. We all nodded hungrily.

Sam led us to the back of a building, where a rusty old motor home was parked. Inside was a small couch and table, and a mini fridge filled with bottles of water and assorted food items, most of which, I was disappointed to see, were some variation on pickled things—pickled herring, pickled eggs, pickled pigs' feet, pickled mushrooms, and even plain, ordinary pickles.

After we had finished choking down our pickled meal, Will slumped onto the couch and let out a long sigh. "So, now that we've saved the world and all, are you guys ready to go home?" he said with a tired smile.

I cleared my throat. "Yeah, um, so about that . . . there's something I need to tell you."

An hour later, the engine of Junkman Sam's motor home spluttered to life. Somewhere out there, six other Ticks would be ready to wipe out the entire population of Earth any day now.

Unless we could stop them.

We rolled out of the compound in silence, unable to put words to what we had just shared.

By the time we reached the interstate, Alicia was perched up front, next to Sam, barking orders in Russian at the rumpled scientist. Will opened and closed a cabinet door compulsively forty-seven times. And me? At the first opportunity, I found myself giving the bathroom door handle a lick.

I guess some things will never change.

But I had a feeling nothing was ever going to be the same again.

From: AwesomeSven@dmail.com
To: SvenCarter@dmail.com

Subject: How's it goin'?

Hey, Weird Sven.

How's it goin'? [Butt Face says, "What's up, my peeps?"]

I hope you had fun in Niagara Falls. Lots has happened since you left. First, I won the school talent show. First prize was $200! It was pretty awesome. Then I tried out for the football team and now I'm the new starting quarterback. Dad says he doesn't know why I'm not so sucky anymore. He says it's like I'm a different Sven.

Mom's going to Tokyo next week. Her salmon-and-brown-sugar chocolate cake recipe was discovered by some Japanese engineers, who found that it's

perfect for plugging up leaks in nuclear
power plants, so they're flying her over
there to help them make a giant batch
of it.

Oh. one more thing. You know that kid
Brandon Marks? Well, he was being kind
of mean. so Butt Face and I pantsed
him in front of the whole school at a
big assembly. He had the biggest poop
stains on his underwear ever! Even the
kids in the back row could see them. So
now everyone calls him Skid Marks. Get
it? Skid marks? He pretty much leaves
us alone now.

Anyway. we're having a great time here.
Don't hurry back.

Sincerely.
Sven

ACKNOWLEDGMENTS
A Play in One Act

ROB VLOCK, *author of* Sven Carter & the Trashmouth Effect, *enters stage left. He crosses half the stage with a purposeful stride before he notices the audience, totally forgets what he was supposed to be doing, and stops. He waves at the audience.*

BRANDON MARKS, *reigning bully at Chester A. Arthur Middle School, enters stage right. Rob is too busy waving to notice Brandon creeping up behind him. With a sudden lunge, Brandon grabs the band of Rob's underwear and executes a vicious wedgie.*

ROB: Alas! I've been wedgied! O, cruel hand of fate that hath yanked my undies unto that celestial realm! Pray tell, vile scoundrel, what ill deed hath wrought such villainy upon mine nethers?

BRANDON: Huh?

ROB: Sorry. It's a play, so I figured we were supposed to be talking like that.

BRANDON: Yeah, no. I'm not talking like that.

ROB: Fine. What I was trying to say was, why did you give me a wedgie?

BRANDON: Like you don't know! It's because you made me look like a big jerk in your stupid book!

ROB: Wait a minute. I wasn't trying to make you look like a jerk. You just ... well, do jerky things sometimes. Or a lot, as the case may be. Anyway, it's not like I didn't have help making this book. There are a ton of people I have to thank for standing behind me when I was writing this. So if you're going to blame me, you have to blame them, too.

BRANDON: Yeah? Well then, it looks like I've got a ton of wedgies to give out. So who's first?

ROB: Well, there's John Rudolph. He's my awesome agent and just a great guy in general. He did a ton to help me make this book better, and he found you and Sven and everyone a great home with an amazing publisher.

BRANDON: John Rudolph, huh? Well, I hope you like wedgies, John. I have a Super Spiral Tighty Whitey with a Half Twist that's got your name all over it.

ROB: And I have to give a whole boatload of thanks to my superstar editor, Amy Cloud, at Aladdin. She's the best! I feel so lucky to be working with her!

BRANDON: A boatload of thanks? I hope she's ready for a *buttload of wedgie*! I'll put her down for an Atomic Peach Pit. Who else?

ROB: There's all the people who read early drafts of my manuscript and give me so much smart, creative feedback along the way. Erin Cashman, Pat Gabridge, Greg Lewis, Diana Renn, Ted Rooney, Julie Wu, Deb Vlock, and Jenny Bent. Thanks, guys!

BRANDON: One Octowedgie coming right up!

ROB: I have to give credit to my parents for making me. And for teaching me to love books and giving me their unconditional support my whole life. I love you, Mom and Dad!

BRANDON: Tell 'em to wear some reinforced underwear. 'Cause there just might be a Boxer Rebellion in their immediate future.

ROB: Thanks to Steve Scott, whose amazing illustration graces the cover of this book!

BRANDON: Steve better be ready to get his drawer's drawers wedged where the sun don't shine. Get it? He's a drawer because he draws things. And drawers is another word for underwear. Get it?

ROB: Uh . . . yeah. Funny. So, moving on. Thanks to my wonderful kids, Max and Immy, for making me fall in love with children's literature and for inspiring me to write a book that will, I hope, make you laugh so hard milk shoots out of your noses.

BRANDON: Max sounds like the perfect kid to try out my latest invention on—the Maximus Gluteus Wedgeus. And Immy? How about a Double Flying Wedge-O-Matic Butter Cutter?

ROB: And an extra-special thanks to Joey, my super-talented wife and best friend in the whole world, who makes me feel incredibly lucky every single day. This book never would have happened without you! I love you!

BRANDON: I *was* going to give her a Spicy Mango Chutney. But you know what? I'd say being married to you is more than punishment enough.

ROB: And, finally, thanks to you. Yes, you—the person who's reading this right now. I hope you've had as much fun reading this book as I've had writing it. You rock!

BRANDON: Ah, yes. *You.* I haven't forgotten about you. Mark my words, dear reader, one of these days, when you least expect it—like when maybe you're eating a peanut-butter-and-jelly sandwich or studying for a big spelling test or playing your favorite video game or just sitting with a finger jammed up your nostril, digging for green gold—*BAM!* You'll find yourself on the receiving end of a wedgie you'll never forget! And who will you have to thank for it? Me, that's who! Bwa-hahahaha! Bwahahahahahaha!

Brandon points right at you and laughs evilly, an icy, bone-chilling cackle that makes your hair stand on end and your butt cheeks clench up in terror. The sound of his laughter echoes through your head as the curtain slowly falls.

THE END

READ ON
for a sneak peek at
Sven's next adventure.

WHO KNEW THAT THE TOUGHEST GIRL I'D ever met would melt into a pile of goo three words into a Dixon Watts song?

Actually, that's not exactly true. She hadn't *entirely* melted into a pile of goo. Because a pile of goo didn't have a right fist that felt like a five-hundred-pound anvil slamming into your face.

I reached this insight—about the anvil, not the goo— the moment Alicia Toth's right fist slammed into my face and felled me as efficiently as Godzilla kicking over a miniature Eiffel Tower made entirely from toothpicks.

I should probably explain. Let me rewind a bit.

* * *

Junkman Sam's ancient motorhome creaked and groaned as it lurched along I-90. Niagara Falls was two hours behind us. Schenectady was two hours ahead.

I stared out the window, even though there was nothing to look at. It wasn't light yet, so the only view I had was the reflection of my own face in the glass. When the occasional car would blow by our slow-moving rust bucket, its headlights washed me out of existence for a moment or two until my face reappeared in the darkened window.

"You're sure he said that, Sven?" Alicia asked for fifth time, her bright green eyes searing into me like a pair of branding irons. "Those were his exact words?"

For the fifth time, I gave her the same answer. "Yes. I'm sure. He asked if I ever wondered why I was called Seven. Then he laughed and said, 'a little something for you to ponder when you think of me.' Only with more stuttering and gurgling because his head was hanging from a gigantic electromagnet."

"You're *sure*?" Alicia repeated.

I sighed and went back to looking out the window. Dr. Shallix, the cybernetic mastermind behind the plot to extinguish every human life on Earth, had been dead for hours. Yet, he still managed to make my life miserable. It wasn't easy coming to terms with the fact that I'd been the intended weapon for Shallix's evil plan.

"Maybe he didn't mean there are other Ticks out there waiting to kill everyone on the planet," Will suggested hopefully. "Maybe he just meant they screwed up the first six Ticks they tried to build. You know, like it took them seven tries to get it right." He ran an oversize hand through his tousled red hair in a way that suggested he didn't believe it himself.

Alicia rounded on him. "And are you willing to bet six billion lives on that?" she snapped.

Before Will could answer, Junkman Sam cleared his throat and called back to us from the driver's seat. "I think it's reasonable to assume that since Sven was designated Seven Omicron, there are other Synthetics like him in the Omicron line."

The color drained out of Will's face. "Wait! You're

saying there are six more Ticks like Sven out there waiting to exterminate all humans?"

Junkman Sam shrugged. "No, I'm not saying that."

A long, relieved sigh escaped Will's lips.

Sam continued. "Could be six more. Could be six hundred. Who knows?"

Will's sigh turned into a kind of strangled moan. He started compulsively flipping an old ashtray open and closed forty-seven times. It was filled with dried up pieces of gum that looked almost as ancient as the RV itself.

That was kind of Will's thing. He had OCD. Obsessive Compulsive Disorder. So when he was scared or stressed or upset, he'd do these little rituals. You know, like turning light switches on and off. Or opening and closing doors. Stuff like that.

Of course, compared to *my* thing, Will's thing was nothing. I ate stuff. Gross stuff. Like, for example, a wad of that old gum stuck in the ashtray Will was messing with. Which, I realized after I popped it in my mouth, tasted a lot like earwax.

"You think they're all programmed to do the same thing as Sven?" Alicia asked, watching me nearly break my teeth on the decades-old gum. "Incubate super viruses that'll wipe out humanity?"

Sam scratched his stubbly chin. "Maybe. They may have mass produced that model and designed each one to function as a disease vector."

Alicia bit her lip nervously. "If there are that many of those things running around, we're in big trouble."

Things. That's what I was. A thing that was made, not born. A weapon. A Synthetic human-like object. Thinking about it made my stomach turn.

I walked to the front of the motorhome and turned on the radio. I just wanted something to listen to other than the present subject of conversation. I didn't care what was on. Anything was better than hearing my friends talk about me like I was a *thing*.

Okay, I take that back.

Because Dixon Watts was singing.

As usual, it sounded just like a cat that had gotten its tail caught in the door.

Girl, you're as fine as some really smooth sandpaper.

I want to kiss your face more than a lightsaber.

I reached out to turn to another station.

Junkman Sam's right hand flew off the steering wheel and slapped my arm away from the radio. "Hey, don't change that! I love this song."

I stared at him like he had just told me his father was an onion bagel. "What? You love this song? Seriously?"

He didn't answer me. Instead, he bobbed his head to the beat and sang along with the train wreck that was coming out of the speakers. "I saw you walking home from the food store! And I knew right then and there you were nude more!"

He was slightly less off-key than Dix Watts.

"You're just joking with me, right?" I asked, somehow knowing he wasn't joking. "I mean, you have to understand just how much this song sucks."

"Dude, shut up!" Will barked. "This tune is awesome!"

Girl, I love you like a dog loves its kibble.

Why can't you love me back just a libble?

"Come on!" I protested. "Listen to it! 'Libble' isn't even a word! He's terrible!"

Alicia scowled at me. "Take that back! Dix is amazing!"

"Yeah, you must be the only person on Earth who doesn't love him!" Will added.

"A few weeks ago you didn't even know who he was!" I countered.

It was true. A month ago, nobody on the planet had heard of Dixon Watts. Then he burst onto the scene like a mushy jack-o-lantern in December, the biggest teen-pop-mega-superstar in the history of music. His song, "Girl, You Are My Shredded Wheat," was at the top spot on every chart in the world. And spots two through twelve on those charts were filled with the other songs from his first album. You couldn't go anywhere without hearing one of those ear-manglers. It was a total nightmare.

"How can you listen to this?" I pressed. "He sounds like blender full of quarters! No, you know what he sounds like? A garbage disposal full of forks. He's the worst singer—"

I didn't get to finish the sentence. Because that was the moment Alicia's anvil of a fist smashed into my face.

The only good thing about being knocked out by Alicia Toth was that I was unconscious for the rest of Dixon Watts's song. When I opened my eyes a few minutes later, I was relieved to hear to the DJ's voice excitedly droning in that slick, plasticky tone pop station radio announcers all like to use.

"That was Dix Watts's mega-super-hit 'Girl, You Are My Shredded Wheat.' But don't you dare turn your radio off! Because we've just gotten a brand-new surprise release from Dix! Here is 'Babe, You Are My Scrambled Eggs'!"

One of the worst things I'd ever heard came warbling out of the RV's speakers.

Babe, you are my scrambled eggs!

I love you and your bacon legs!

I got unsteadily to my feet. "Oh, man! Not another one! Haven't I suffered enough?" I blurted through a fat lip, instantly wishing I could bite back the words as I thought about Alicia's fist and its run-in with my face.

So just relax and don't put up a fight.

'Cause you know it's gonna be all right.

But Alicia didn't respond at all. No one did. Alicia, Will and Sam all just sat perfectly still, frozen in concentration. Like the tentacles of that awful tuneless abomination playing on the radio had wormed their way through the woofers and tweeters to burrow directly into my friends' brains.

It was almost like they were in a trance.

I cleared my throat. "Uh, guys?" I said tentatively.

They ignored me.

"Guys!" I shouted. "Are you okay?"

Will turned and fixed a pair of glazed eyes on me. "Okay? Yeah. Better than okay. Amaaaaazing."

He said the words flatly, mechanically, drawing out the final *A* like it was an ice cream cone he was savoring.

"Will? What's going on? A few minutes ago you were about to have a total freakout about the other Ticks out there. Now you're amazing?"

"Ticks?" Alicia intoned emotionlessly. "You know, I've been thinking they're not all that bad. I don't know why we were all worried about them."

Something was definitely wrong with them! Alicia's parents died at the hands of Ticks back when she lived at the Settlement in the Chernobyl exclusion zone. And you saw how she got when I insulted a song she liked. So there was no way the Alicia I knew would say Ticks weren't all that bad. What was going on here?

Yeah, don't hate, don't fight, don't push, don't shove.

Just have a stack of pancake love.

The song! That horrifically awful song! It was doing something to the others!

I grabbed Will by the shoulders and shook him. "Will! Come on! Wake up! Hey!"

But he just stared straight ahead with a half-smile on his face.

"Alicia!" I cried. "Alicia, are you with me?"

I slapped her. Normally, something like that probably would have resulted in one or more of my bones being broken. But all Alicia did was sing along with the chorus:

Babe, you are my scrambled eggs!

I love you and your bacon legs!

Oooo-kay.

Let's try plan B.

Turn off the radio.

I reached for the volume knob.

Without warning, Junkman Sam sprang from his seat and tried to wrestle me away from the radio, his sweat-stained armpit pressing damply against my ear as he clamped me into a headlock.

I'd had just enough time to realize that this left nobody driving the motorhome when the vehicle swerved to the right, plowed through a guardrail, bounced its way down an embankment and slammed directly into a tree.